THE LOST CRYSTAL OF LEN

[The Lanterncup series]

ISBN 978-0-9964830-0-1

90000

Author: Marcus Tay (11 years old)

Printed in the United States of America

@2015 Tay's Imagination World.

All rights reserved

ISBN #: 978-0-9964830-0-1

Adolko — The Northern Hemisphere

Shadow Clan Territory

Land of No-purpose
Pya
Arctic Reef
Cold Dunes
Faysa
Kakutah

Tropical Fruit Plantation
outstretched land

Lar
Toosh
CooC
Goliather's Lair

Motique
Dop

Teer
Farmland
Tache
Mt. ORSO
Kahocca
North Pole
Yart
Gulf of Massive Ice Craters
Forest of Traps
Mocha
Tapwa
cove

Wall Line Moor
TAKSO
I.T.I.C.
Yun
Saik

Underwater Volcanoes

Jungle of Mazes

Island of perfection
eeeto

Desert of Longing

Sand Bay
Plaine Wreckage

Land of Secrets

— The Mountain of Day and Night
FFFFF Bistro
Tad
unknown
Roost
Kae

Terp
Gtekin
Wool Islands
Crent

Lotan
Rolathaih
Crotan
Teek

equator Line

Wasteland of Hardships
Forbidden Landscape
zark

Contents:

Prologue: A Little Conversation

A rasping voice cried, "We need...the crystal!" He banged his hand against the table top, smashing the glass to bits and creating a web of cracks. "Would someone please lend me an idea to a successful mission of snatching the object without the legendary beasts noticing??"

The colonel walked by and took a seat across his cruel leader. He squeezed between the arm rests as the fancy chair itself squeaked.

"My majesty, your terrorizing process is going by very well," the colonel smiled crookedly. "I expect double the work of today by tomorrow!" His Majesty exclaimed, with hatred in his voice. "Well then, do you still find my reporting credible?" the colonel questioned smoothly. "Yes, I sure do," His Majesty said. He changed the topic.

"Partly, I've been wondering how my forces can get themselves in the mountain at the far-corner of the northwest. How would they not awaken the three beasts from out of the depths," he spoke. "Give me time to ponder," the colonel told him as he threw a mint into his mouth. There were several minutes of silence.

"I know!" the colonel finally exclaimed. "Do you remember Cliff??" "Say who?" "Cliff, oops, I mean Clive," he corrected himself. "Yeah, what about him??" His Majesty inquired. "Listen attentively," the colonel ordered. "Ok."

"Nowadays, Clive has a descendant named Arnold, who beget een, I mean Ian," he spoke. The colonel stretched out his own tongue and started doing exercises with it.

His Majesty wasn't amused with the pause and threw an apple cutter at the colonel, it went straight into the upper half of his arm and created an artwork of cuneiform.

The colonel tore it off adamantly, grinding his teeth. He glanced at His Majesty, but just sighed. "Are you going to continue??" His Majesty questioned. The colonel nodded.

"Do not get stubborn or dismayed, I will continue," he noted swiftly. The colonel took a deep breath.

"I was thinking that you should pay them a visit and murder the head of the household, Arnold. That would make Worry, no, I mean, Lorry, become aware of us and order Ian to retrieve the crystal. He wouldn't know his final destination has beasts 100 times larger than him," the colonel said thoughtfully.

"What if he fails? There is a good chance he would! I don't find this credulous, but I'll still implement your idea. I certainly like how someone else does the job for us, not even knowing it," His Majesty exclaimed.

In the meantime, as he makes his journey, I'll put many handy traps before him. Who knows, he might even fall off track and die!" His Majesty chuckled.

"I have reason to do this because I love testing my opponents. Also, because only a tad of me really believes he is going to make it."

"What if he gets escorted by allies?" the colonel asked apprehensively. His Majesty still looked satisfied. "Then, let them bring it on!" His Majesty broke into laughter.

Chapter One: The Surprise

The wind howled, trees swayed, leaves trembled, grass rustled. It was a windy fall morning, about four o'clock. Apparently, that meant wake-up time for Ian Lanterncup.

His alarm clock woke him with a start, almost giving him a stroke as usual. As he sprawled on his bed, Ian kept thinking of his yesterday's feast at a buffet.

The buffet had a variety of soups that Ian loved, but he favored one the most. "Peppered Tomato and Cream Cheese," Ian whispered.

It might sound disgusting to you, but it was flavored with much more than what its name spoils. Ian had smelled and tasted condiment including lime basil.

Ian had filled the liquid up to the rim, and after finishing it, his own body went into a series of hiccups. That was the only not-good part. He couldn't get up for a second round just because of that.

But after it ceased, the buffet was already closing for the night. They were addressed to get out with excuses by the manager probably because her employees were tired and needed rests.

She had said something about a fire occurring in the kitchen, but Ian doubted it because of her tone and behaver. She had shooed them right out an emergency exit.

Ian brushed the top of his half brown and half yellowish hair. He always admired his own hair. As a clump, it was puffy unlike when it was contaminated with gel.

Ian and his mom always stirred up angry disputes over different types of coiffures when Ian had to go to a wedding and even the theater. It was a conspicuously bad subject to create a whole fuss about with somebody else opposing you.

He got up with a heave and touched the window with all five fingers. Wow, he thought, as a chill went up his body. It was so cold that if you keep your hand pressed against the window for even ten seconds, your hand is likely to change its color to red in an instance. Even in the fall, the harsh winter seemed to drag on.

Ian glanced outside through his octagon-shaped window at several moose with antlers (were everywhere in the North) that paced in circles.

He also saw hens walking on their property, their heads bobbing frontwards and backwards, never side to side. They apparently were tearing of pieces of grass and swallowing it despite having no teeth to crunch and chew.

He averted his eyes and saw mist encasing the trunk of an oak tree, its branches careening. What bothered Ian was how the mist seemed to change both color and shape outside. Oh, come on Ian, you have to stop worrying about this nonsense, he told himself.

His family lived on a twenty-acre piece of land his great-great-grandfather had earned for helping the queen of Tapwa carry out duties. They lived in a city state named Yart.

Ian craned his neck and did some indoor daily warm-ups he had been practicing for weeks. He did wall-sits, jumping jacks, and sit-ups to try to keep fit. Ian wondered how people did cartwheels, he wasn't acrobatic.

Ian strolled back to his queen-sized bed, collapsing on it even though he was fully awake already. Ian set himself downright and pulled the covers over him. Ian recalled good times when he was just a toddler. He lay in thoughts.

Two hours later (finally) his parents woke up. Ian's dad, Arnold Lanterncup, and Ian's mom, Lorry Lanterncup, yawned so loud that the blue jays outside threw into a panic, that caused cacophony.

Ian barged out of his room and bumped into his father. Arnold looked at down at him and smirked. Ian smiled back, relieved to see his own father happy again after the death of his older brother which Ian only met twice.

"How was your night's sleep, son," Arnold asked, with not much enthusiasm. Well, Ian thought, he asks the same question every day. "It was good," which was the answer he also gave back, every day.

His dad studied him for a few awkward moments, but then it was intercepted with a clap from his mother (which was done to get either Ian or his dad to pay attention, immediately).

"Ian dear, please meet me downstairs in five minutes so I can explain about the secrets of your ancestor that I have been avoiding to tell you for years."

Chapter Two: The Shortened Story and the Save

"Your great-great-great-great-great-great-great-great-great-great-great-great-great-great-great-great-great-great-great-great grandfather," "how many greats was that again?" "Twenty, and no more interruptions," snapped his mother.

"Ok," said Ian. His mom continued. "Your many greats grandfather was named Clive." "Clive what?" "Lanterncup, you dummy!! Did I say NO interruptions?!" "Fine, fine," Ian grumbled.

"Clive was a dragon trainer, warrior, and a brave man." Yeah, I hear that a lot in bedtime stories, Ian thought. His mom yet continued.

"How Clive's dad went missing is still a conundrum to this day. Supposedly he died in the war against the dragons, but we don't have records of that." "What a war," Ian interrupted once again. "Zah!!" Lorry exclaimed.

"But if it was such a big war why didn't they record it? And if it was a war with the dragons, why was he a dragon trainer? And…." "Stop," Lorry ordered, interrupting Ian's tirade of questions.

"One question at a time please, but to answer your questions, they didn't record it because that was 2000 years ago, you dum-dum. And he was a dragon trainer because he made peace! He fought other creatures like monsters and wild beasts that were not dragons," Lorry explained.

"Like that one?" Ian said worriedly as he saw the mist outside grin in an odd way. Arnold barged right into their conversation and said, "You told him the truth?" "Yes, but look out!" Ian and Lorry both cried.

Arnold turned his body without lifting up his ankle in a 180 degree. With quick reflexes, he attempted to parry the sword that flew straight-on at Ian. It was thrown by a shimmering figure just outside the window, who was made-up of what Ian had been feeling apprehensive about; the mist.

The sword went crashing through the window. Arnold's attempt was abortive. With a whistling sound, the tip of the sword sank into Arnold's abdomen. He crumbled.

"NO!" Ian cried. Lorry took out what Ian guessed was an ice sword and pointed it at the ghostly figure. "Begone," she screamed. With an evil grin, the phantom dissolved. Ian's curiosity took him over. "How did you do that?" "It doesn't matter," his mom said.

She turned to Arnold, who lay on the floor clutching his abdomen with both hands. He had lost way too much blood. "Arnold, you cannot leave now." "I must, sweet heart, it is my destiny," Arnold stammered with a final breath. He fainted with Lorry sobbing at his knees.

Ian ran for bandages, but he knew it was too late. Then, he got mad at himself. Why did I not tie up his wound earlier? Ian thought. He started to go into shock.

Ian banged his head against a mirror and started crying. Then everything went black as the mailman knocked on the door and saw them all passed out through a first floor window. He dialed 911.

Chapter Three: Hospitalized

Ian awoke slowly with blurry vision, "Where am I? Is my dad okay?" he heard muttering. "Can anyone hear me?" More muttering.

"Hi-yah," Ian attempted to do a Chinese Getup, but halfway up, pain came rushing in his back. There was a harsh-sounding CRAACK! All he saw was a sign saying Yart Hospital.

"Doctor, doctor," said a nurse outside in the corridor, "I heard an unpleasant sound!" Dr. Kim came jogging down from the east building, "Sorry I'm late for my afternoon shift."

Then, a food cart filled with trays of fresh goodies turned a corner, and the doctor crashed and tumbled over it, spilling orange juice and chicken noodle soup (that was what patients were supposed to chow down).

"That food was expensive," the manager shouted angrily, "you are FIRED!" "But I have to attend to my patient!" Dr. Kim protested. "Fine, but you're on probation," the manager cried adamantly.

Dr. Kim walked into room 49 and heard Ian groaning. "I will be right there." "Ah-glah," Ian replied. Dr. Kim pulled the curtain back. "My-y-y b-a-a-ck." The doctor examined him. "Looks like you need surgery, young man," he said. "No, ah-ah," gurgled Ian. With all his might, Ian spoke. "Tak mee too mi da," (take me to my dad).

✳ ✳ ✳

As Ian rolled into room 54 on his wheelchair, the zig-zaggy lines on the screen arrived at a straight line. Ian took a deep breath. Crying will not help, he thought. But his emotions fought back. Tears rained down his face.

"Here, eat this," a man said. Ian could have literally jumped out of his untied shoes if it was not for the clasp on his shoulder.

Ian spun his wheelchair with moderate speed and examined the guy. He had wispy dirty-blond hair, and wore simple clothes of tattered khakis and an orange t-shirt. The guy was like in his early 40's. At least it looked like it.

"Janitor Joe, why are you here," Ian said with surprise. "No questions, eat first," Joe thrust a lemon sour candy pack into his hands.

"Hey," Ian remembered, "do you happen to know where my mom is??" "Oh yes," Joe replied, "she is at the recovery room." "Thanks," said Ian.

"Thing is, I cannot get up and walk because I have just been through a quick little surgery." "Little?" Joe inquired. "Uh, yes," Ian confirmed.

"Can I push you then?" Joe asked. "Well, think about it, if there is too much pressure on my back, wouldn't it be painful for me?" "Yes, yes, I suppose so."

Ian couldn't blame Janitor Joe for not knowing common sense and having a callow concept. The guy had been kicked out of every unpopular college school in the continent.

Chapter Four: Back to School

After a week's recovery, Ian was good to go. The nurse asked him how was the condition on one of those face scales, and Ian said three, which meant a little tear streaming down its cheek. One point is that, he hated shots. Ian hated them because they were like pinches (he got a lot at school).

At 11:00 am, he stood up for the first time in a week. Oh, oh, it felt so relieving and pacifying. He thanked everyone who kept him feel at home, and put down how well the service was on a piece of paper (10/10).

"I feel so fresh," he told the manager, who tried avoiding him, but it didn't work. "Do a favor for me, give your employees a raise." The manager rolled his eyes, and uttered, "If I happen to do so."

Ian skipped to the nearest elevator and pressed the "down" button. Ding! The doors slid open. He descended to the main lobby and walked happily out.

Ian had no idea why he was so happy. Maybe it was……aha! His two best friends Drake Voulcaner and Alexis Vos were slumped on couches facing the west wing. They did not seem to notice him. "Hey guys, hey guys!" Ian could not be happier. He ran towards them, just to topple a fake tree.

All heads turned his way. "Uh, hey," it was a common way to respond. Who knows why? Everyone just went back to their business.

Alexis helped him up, and Drake embraced him with a hug, "Oh, man, what happened?" Ian told them everything, from start to finish, which took him at least ten minutes. When he was done, his friends were speechless and seemed to have been infected with aphasia.

"W-o-w," Alexis stammered. "Y-yes," Drake agreed. "My question is, who is this freak who killed my father?" "NO idea," they both said at the same time.

Just when Ian was reaching boiling temperature, Janitor Joe appeared at the main entrance, "I am you people's personal taxi driver, okay?" Joe the toilet bowl cleaner called from the main entrance. "Yeah, that's fine," Drake blurted out.

Da-da-doo-doo-tee....yah. Music boomed out of the radio. Joe had rolled down the windows and increased the volume to max. "Aaack," Ian cried. "Do we have to listen to this Mexican dance?" Alexis cried out. "It's not that bad," Drake called from the passenger seat, "I love it!" "What?" Alexis yelled uncomfortably. "Don't worry, we are getting there," Joe called from the front.

After fifteen minutes, a brick building came into view. Yes, yes, thought Ian. A sign read: Yart Northern School. Joe parked near a sign that read: School Worker Lots, and shut the car down.

✳✳✳

As Ian reached out his hand to turn the doorknob of his math classroom, he froze because a voice shouted out of the speaker in the hallway. "Hello, this is Principal Boris, and I want Ian Lanterncup to report to my office immediately." "WE are going with you," said Alexis.

Just then, the bully and nicknamed Patrick the Pink Pincher, A.K.A., Josh, paced out the door. "Oh, there you are, you later loser." Ian clenched his fingers tightly.

"It doesn't even make sense, and what you said was unreasonable!" Ian put on a bad-guy-get-lost stare he had been practicing. "Oh, don't give such a facial expression, you are just stressed-out because you dream too much!" What? Ian almost screamed it out, but he knew better than to.

Josh was a guy with frizzly brown hair who loved to wear sandals (all the time) with a red shirt and dark trousers.

"We better get going," Drake said. He took both Ian and Alexis's arms and pulled them away down the north corridor. "Where is Joe?" Ian questioned. "Cleaning sinks," answered Drake.

A minute passed as they made their way to Principal Boris' office, passing the cafeteria, music room, school auditorium, theater, planetarium, and drama stage. "Looks like we are getting another two-hour detention," Alexis pointed out. "Yup," Ian substantiated.

At last, they made it. A sign read: NO to everything you ask me, I make my own regulations and protocols.

Ian ringed the bell, no answer. He ringed again. A short stout man peered through the door, "Hello, sorry, but, your buds are prohibited." "What!" Drake screeched. "Yes, I am sorry for inconvenience, but this is private," Boris said smoothly. Drake heaved a sigh. "Tis okay," Ian reminded him. "Be careful what you say," Alexis reminded Ian. He walked in without a glance back.

Boris yawned and stretched, which made Ian sick. "Tell me, why have you been absent a week without contacting me?" Ian gulped, "I was hospitalized." "What?!" "Yeah," Ian corroborated. "Listen, I just want this to be quick and short," said Boris firmly. "Huh?" Ian was perplexed.

Suddenly, the strangest (and most uncommon) thing happened in Ian's life. His (thought he knew) principal slowly transformed into a creature so horrifying it could make you keep taking deep breaths and saying "Please" with hands ready to block.

"What the heck," Ian screamed. He ran to the door. Click! Ian forgot that his principal had a button he could simply press to lock the door on both sides.

Ian turned around to see that his principal had grown four feet taller. So, he was now nine feet.

Alexis pounded on the door. "Are you ok in there?" Ian wanted to answer, but for some reason, he couldn't. Was his heartbeat gradually getting faster until it reached its climax?

Here is some quick description of what Ian saw of the creature from his perspective. Tentacles. Dozens of them protruding from main tentacles connected to the back of his shoulder blades. Another observation, fiery mouth. No wonder every time Ian saw Principal Boris eat an apple, the apple seemed to get brighter. His skin was purple. Also, he had dinosaur legs and webbed feet. Everything else looked normal.

"I am, The Shocker," he cackled. Ian screamed like a little kid you has just woken up from a nightmare. He did some quick thinking. He thought of techniques. Hmmm, "aha."

"What are you going to do," The Shocker derided. "A technique I learned in science class," Ian cried frantically.

He charged, and head-butted The Shocker in the belly. "Ahgu," The Shocker gurgled. "Oh, I am not done," Ian tried anxiously to do a round kick, but unfortunately lost his balance.

Pain swelled into him right after impact with the floor. "No," Ian groaned. "Yes, oh yes," The Shocker hissed. A split second later, electricity sparkled from his tentacles. "I am literally The Shocker," he cried.

Ian was impotent. This is the end, he thought. No one will ever know what happened to me. He thought of wall-blasting his way out, but Ian was dubious it would work.

It happened so fast that his mind didn't react. Ian stood up and discovered that the door had slammed right into The Shocker.

"Ian, Ian," came the voice of Joe Bark. "Here," Ian called, "we have to get out of here and.....RUN!"

Ian took off, only to trip over a wire connected to a vacuum cleaner right outside the office. Janitor Joe came into focus. "Sorry about that," he said.

With his large right hand, Joe scooped up Ian's legs and dragged him, still sprinting, while Ian was still face down on the ground. Ian found it hard to talk, but he managed to say a phrase, "Whar ees tham," (where is them). "In the cafeteria," Joe replied. "O," Ian gagged.

Joe pelted threw hallway after hallway, finally reaching the cafeteria.

"You two, listen up. I want you both to follow me to the Janitor's chamber." "What?" Drake shouted. "Just do it." In the background, the sound of The Shocker grew louder. "Come out, come out, where ever you are." Great, they thought.

Unfortunately, The Shocker found them near the board room.

He did not have to walk, seeing that The Shocker had tentacles that worked exactly like feet, but on walls. "Wallker" would have been another good name for him. "I will and shall destroy you all," The Shocker taunted.

Joe back-peddled and turned a corner. "You cannot escape me," The Shocker cried out. "We WILL get out of here," Janitor Joe yelled back.

After a few turns, Joe charged through a wooden door with stains, hauling Ian onto his back at the same time. Joe held the door opened as Alexis and Drake ran in, while The Shocker screamed colorfully.

"Did we lose him?" Alexis wondered. "I think so," Joe made an approving face, but it didn't lighten their hopes. "All righty, give us a tour of this wonderful place, Joe," Drake said sarcastically.

Ian grabbed the nearest sponge, not even considering if it was washed before, and started scrubbing his own face.

Thin layers of the wall stood peeled and hanging as they trudged through the Janitor's workshop. Dim lights shone from various candles strapped to the ceiling. Murky water puddles appeared once in a while on the ground.

"Ugh, how much longer?" Drake called exhaustedly. "Be patient," Joe answered. "Why are we even doing this?" Drake argued, "I mean, this is pointless right?" "Not quite," Joe responded calmly.

About five and a half minutes (Ian was not sure) later, the school janitor pushed against a section of wall. Somehow, a door resembled, and moved inward, then aside, like it was welcoming them. The room inside was pitch black.

"You sure it's safe?" Ian popped up. All three of them turned toward him and looked at him like he was a disgrace. "Why would Joe take us to a harmful place," Alexis said back. "Well...," Ian had tons of reasons, but he knew not to continue.

Joe flicked on the lights and exclaimed, "ta-da!" He outstretched his hand like whatever was in front of them, was a masterpiece. "What is that?" Drake inquired curiously. In the center stood something that looked like a refrigerator. Instead, it glowed, and was wider.

Joe gave Alexis the measuring tape, and she excitedly took it. Alexis ran to the object, and measured its height and width. "Let us see," she started. "Six foot six for the height, and seven foot two for the width." Ian always thought Alexis was a math genius. "Ok," Drake whistled.

The room was made of a combination of bedrock and granite. It was approximately just eight feet tall, and eleven feet across.

The chamber was vacant and only contained the like-refrigerator object that stood like a statue in the middle and a wooden wardrobe in the corner. There was nothing else, only blank space.

"Do you usually go in here?" Drake questioned. "Not a whole lot. Besides, I have only been here twice," Joe said. "When was the last time you came in," Ian asked. "Exactly one year ago," Joe replied. "I found a wedge in the wall, so I peered through and saw something bright."

"Of course, I wanted to check it out, even though I didn't know what it was. You know, I got my first medal for being the most curious boy in my elementary school which I gotten expelled from at third grade."

"Tell me about it," Alexis begged. "Long story, it will take me a day," Joe responded. "But now, Ian, you get the honors to open the doors."

Ian was stunned. He never got honors and fame and attention. Ian was a plain old dude who needed to work on his handwriting and spelling.

"Come on," Joe urged, "You've got it. The case of Vapdello won't bite." "Wait, what," Ian called, as he approached the thing. "I never said anything," Joe called back. Ian wondered if that was his imagination. Or was it some ghost who spoke into his ear?

When finally Ian reached the case, he gripped his hands on both handles and pulled. Light blinded him before he could shield himself.

Chapter Five: The Flashback

It was the first day of summer break, and Ian sat with his little cousin, Jarret, who was only seven years old, under an oak tree in the forest south of Yart on stumps.

They sat near the riverbank on smooth rocks covered with minerals. The warm breeze and the fresh smell of The Kiffe River was very wonderful. Dragonflies flew in circles on top of other oak trees.

Ian had just finished telling Jarret an anecdote which he found really fascinating. Every time Ian finished a sentence, there would be an ovation coming from one person.

They had planned their day. First, to experience nature at the forest. Second, to get ice cream. Third, to fish. And finally, go biking.

Even though they lived in the north close to Glacier Kingdom, the summer was pretty intense. Ian was allowed to go on his own with Jarret because he proved to be a matured guy in the last few weeks.

"Ian, over here," came the voice of Arnold Lanterncup. "What!" Ian was too distracted to realize that his dad was peeking out of the side of a mulberry tree on the other side of the river. "Oh, there you…why did you come?" Ian said with disbelief. "I had to as a father," answered Arnold. "Listen, something is strange about this place." "No way," Ian argued. "Just get over here quickly." "Fine," sighed Ian, "as you wish. Jarret, we are going to cross that bridge, okay?" "Yeah," Jarret replied.

Halfway across, a dozen figures seemed to materialize out of the oak trees behind them. Arnold ran out of his hiding spot with a curved sword that pirates used towards the enemy. "Hurry, get across, I knew something was coming," Arnold yelled.

Ian sprinted to the other side, momentarily forgetting to pull Jarret along. The seven year old stood as a block of ice on the bridge.

"Jarret, what are you doing?" Ian shouted worriedly. "I know what they want," Jarret started speaking, staring down at the rushing water that lapped on gigantic rocks in the river.

"I must die." "Are you crazy?" "No, I'm not," Jarret responded confidently.

"I shall jump, it's the only way they will go." "How do you know all this?" "I just know."

Jarret jumped. Ian saw his spirit leave his body right before it disappeared in the water. The figures vaporized.

Chapter Six: High-Speed Chase

"Ian, wake up," Alexis' voice came from far away, "you have got to see this." That made him fully conscious again as he awoke with tears streaming down his cheeks. He realized he was back in the chamber with the refrigerator thingy.

Ian sat up hastily. "It's okay, you are fine," Alexis said, sitting at hero position on the ground. Drake supported him up. Joe was examining objects from the case that were....weapons?

There was a whole assortment of guns, swords, gadgets, and many other cool stuff. "Whoa," Ian said with awe. "Let's see, try this," Joe handed him a hand/arm shaped thing that was way too high-tech. It had two curved knives protruding from an opening in the front. "It's called the Wrist Striker 280," Joe noted.

"Why 280?" Ian inquired. Joe shrugged, "That is what the label reads." "There are labels in the case?" "Yes," Joe replied.

Ian tried playing with it. "How do you put it on," cried Ian. "You don't know?" Joe said, "You really do need to learn to be autonomous. Even I am better than you." "Oh come on! I wasn't born with that kind of talent!" "It's not a talent!" Joe screamed. "Fine, let us adjourn this altercation," Ian begged. Joe eyed him grimly and glanced away.

It was true. Joe was born to be a handyman and hard-worker. He was even starting to get little biceps and triceps despite his 33cm waist. Even though he had a calorie-burning job, hamburgers for lunch and snack every day beat it.

Joe hobbled over and fit the gadget around Ian's hand in a matter of thirteen seconds. "Perfect," exclaimed Joe. "Nice," Drake called with amazement. "You will need it," Alexis added.

Ian averted his eyes to where Drake and Alexis were checking out weapons in front of the case.

"Hey, I think Josh would be real jealous if we showed-off our gear and also not tell him where we got them," Ian teased. "Yup, how I long to see him beg with promises that he can't keep," Drake replied.

After a few minutes of trying new body armor, Ian heard Drake howl excitedly. "Check this out." Drake spun a glade into the air, and as it spiraled down, it could have decapitated him if Joe hadn't caught it, inches from his face.

Everyone held their breath as Drake went to a corner and huddled up by squeezing his knees to his chest and rocking back and forth. Ian could almost feel how close Drake got to a panic attack. How close he could have died, a horrible death.

Awkward silence.

Joe finally broke it. Not with words, but with action. He stomped over to a wooden wardrobe, where he took out his mop. With it, he twirled the mop, and then, to Ian's amazement, turned into a staff with a gap on the top. "Is anything supposed to fit right into that little hole?" "Yes, but it's missing." "How?" "I'll explain later," said Joe monotonously.

This time, Joe smacked the staff on the wall, and it transformed into a rifle in less than a second. Ian raised his hand. "Yes?" "Uh, did this case just appeared here?" "Yeah," Joe picked up a cloth and wiped his face with it.

"Then, don't you want to know why or how?" Alexis interrupted. "Listen youngling, I am not those who try to find answers and unlock mysteries. I simply just take into use what I discover." "Oh," Alexis responded glumly.

"Anyway, I can't find a type of melee that suits me," Alexis told Joe unhappily. "Naw, you will find something, even though....you sure nothing catches your eyes in this package?" Drake suddenly stepped out of the darkness (at least that was what Ian thought) and gave them all a millisecond heart attacks.

"I have got to say, Joe, you saved my life!" "Ugh, you thank me now?" Joe chuckled. They both laughed (a long time).

Finally, Joe remembered the situation they were in. "We should go and confront The Shocker and make our escape now." "What!" Ian felt guilty for blurting that out. "You sure the police don't have him on the ground already," Drake shouted.

Joe narrowed his right eye, leaving his left in the same place. "Ok, that's creepy," was Drake's response. Joe turned his head this time.

"Hey, take the glade." "No, I cannot." "You must," Joe said sternly. Now Drake took it. "What about me," Alexis piped up. "I, Joe Bark, shall cover you." "KK."

Ian had enough time to gather up his courage until Joe front-kicked the door to the Janitor's closet wide open. Natural light bursts in from the nearest window. Ian, Drake, and Alexis, had to squint at first glance.

"Follow me," Joe whispered. They managed to make it to the cafeteria when Joe stopped abruptly. "What," Ian started. "Listen," Joe urged.

The Shocker's voice boomed from a....microphone? "As you see, I have locked every single exit in the school, and in the meanwhile, let's play a game of Treasure Hunt with your hands tied together. The one who finds Ian Lanterncup and his unfortunate devoted followers will be spared. But first, you will all have to watch a little show I prepared," he spoke smoothly.

Ian risked a peek as Alexis grunted and said, "He is talking about you." What Ian saw was too horrifying. All the teachers of the school were monsters! Sluggish creatures. All the students had their hands tied back behind their chairs, so it looked like it was part of their bodies. And there he was, Josh, with masking tape over his mouth, he spluttered gibberish.

With his humanoid left hand, The Shocker pulled Josh's chair to the center of the room, where there was a tiny circle. The tables just disappeared. "You will all experience the reason why you should fear me, right now," tentacles reached slowly toward Josh.

Some students tried shutting down their sense of sight for a moment, but the sluggish creatures kept their eyes open with their pincers (those slugs' hands).

Ian couldn't bear seeing any of his classmates die a gruesome death. He threw himself into a sprint, jumped over chairs as if they were hurtles, and karate-chopped his history teacher with the keen end of a piece of metal sticking out of his Wrist Striker. She melted into molasses stuff.

"All right, Lanterncup, you have returned," The Shocker spat, "but you are too late to save your arch-enemy." "No, I am not!" Ian pressed a random button on his Wrist Striker as tentacle one neared Josh's shoulder.

"Aha!" Ian kicked The Shocker in his right shin, and then shot a bolt of fire from his gadget. It went through the wall, creating an aperture.

"Reinforcements, I need more Sloogpaps," The Shocker cried. The Sloogpaps closed in on him. There were about nine.

Then, Joe charged in and saved the day with Drake behind. "Nice grand opening," Joe shouted. Joe was boss. He dodged pincers and swiped and did some cool moves. "Beat that, caterpillars." Ian could tell that those creatures suddenly had red-hot faces, and knew instantly that they were offended.

That was how they got Joe of his feet. Alexis ran in, surprising three Sloogpaps, and dragged Joe back to where they started. "Drake," Ian called, "we should escape now." "Oh, right,"

Drake did his best doing the limbo under one of those creature's arm, and pelted to the opposite end where Joe had just recovered.

"One word, RUN!!" That was Joe's call. It felt like slow motion for some time as they wisped passed corridor and corridor.

Yes, thought Ian, the front door. They burst into broad daylight and fresh air, where Ian just wanted to lie down and get tan.

Halfway across the parking lot to Joe's van, The Shocker and his minions threw the door at a pedestrian who dodged right in time.

"Get in, get in," Joe cried worriedly. "But Joe, you haven't even clicked on your car keys yet," Alexis said. "Darn," he rummaged in his shirt pocket and thankfully found it.

Joe shut on the car, and not caring to backup, drove right over the curb, almost running over a random citizen in a business suit.

Even worse, they found themselves at oncoming traffic. "Ah," Ian screamed. "Turn, turn, turn," Drake screamed. He hauled himself up from the back seat and reached for the wheel.

"No! We won't die like this," Joe said with controlled tone.

Ian had to contemplate what happened next. Let's see. There was a loud SCREECH, and it felt as like the world just lost gravity for one second. In the back trunk, the glass shattered into thousands of pieces when a SUV crashed.

As Ian blinked the dots out of his eyes, he saw that three ordinary-sized brown jeeps with headlights the size of elephants, were followed by two helicopters and ten police cars through the mirror.

Joe headed straight to a tunnel which will bring them into the city of Yart. "Why are you crazily-driving into a city of four million people," cried Alexis. "We have to react fast in these situations," Joe answered.

But then, a man's head popped out of an opening on the top of the jeep in the middle. He opened fire with a rapid-firing gun that Ian didn't recognize.

Little sparkles glittered on the shield of Joe's car. Pretty soon the paint would go off as Joe moved from lane to lane on the main highway of Yart. In the distance, the city stood like standing-up fries ready to be toasted with gunpowder.

WHAM! The helicopter on the right descended towards Joe's Honda, twirling awkwardly. Ian saw steam protruding from the engine and the back of the tail. Then, Ian had a clear sight of a man with six-pack abs, and of course, a rocket launcher.

"If we don't zip past into that tunnel before the helicopter hits, we will be stuck by an object-made cul-de-sac," Drake shouted.

The light of the sun flashed, tree leaves swayed, all created things seemed to be focused on speed.

Vroom! The sound of friction hit Ian's ears really hard that he had to yelp. They actually passed into the tunnel as Ian looked at the driver's rear mirror and saw flames erupt.

Drake slumped forward and was relieved instantly. He didn't look as apprehensive as before, when they were in school.

Drake's hand went to his pocket, slipping out a pair of sunglasses. He handed one to Ian, who sat across from him because Alexis occupied the middle one.

"Hey, how come I don't get to have one?" Alexis inquired unhappily. "The sun, its heat is by far very intense!" Drake shrugged, "Sorry about that, I forgot to buy...."

There was a ROOM, and one of the same jeeps that went after them had driven through the now-useless body of the burning helicopter and flew into midair.

It scraped the ceiling of the tunnel, leaving a mark, and fell vertically down onto the road, almost smashing a car which honked angrily at it, dodging out of the way.

Joe did some crazy movement with the wheel, turning it sideways and knocking a random car into the wall.

"Sorry!" Joe muttered. He stared at the wheel once again, concentrating. "Aha!"

Joe turned it at about 35 degrees to the other side, making the car move through two lanes. He apparently was breaking the law by driving on a yellow line.

Joe made hand gestures to try to convince cars in front of him to diverge so he could drive through. Unfortunately, they didn't really want to listen to his commands. So he came up with an excellent idea.

Joe tore open a bag in his car as he kept his foot on the pedal. He rummaged in it and snatched out a mini disco ball. Joe stuck it to the front window with its rubber bottom.

He pressed a button on it with one hand and suddenly a series of rainbow-colored light shown on solid surfaces.

Drivers averted their eyes and saw the colorful lights, suddenly mistaken that Joe was a cop chasing a criminal who jacked someone's owned car from a dealership.

They hurriedly drove to either one side or the other, letting Joe pass. Ian stared with awe at the sight of strangers opening up a path for them.

Joe's car quickly went straightforward, passing the speed limit on a sign that was at the entrance of the tunnel.

Not only did they let them pass, but they also let the jeep go too. "You fools!" Ian, Drake, and Alexis groaned as they glanced backwards through the opening in the damaged trunk.

They made it out of the tunnel, partly relieved to be out of the underground.

Joe hastily parked his car in a lot near a toy store and yelled, "Come on, come on, out!" "No way Joe," Ian shouted, "I am not escaping by foot!" "Now, you be flexible and not lazy! Do not negotiate with me or protest!" Joe demanded and ordered.

Ian obeyed and abruptly pushed the door open, but he fell and smacked his head on the curb, connected to both the sidewalk and the dried-tar road. It was excruciatingly painful.

"Get up!" Joe urged. He sighed and lifted Ian onto his shoulders, overwhelmed and tired.

Alexis took the lead with Drake back-upping her. Together, Joe and the two of them sprinted down the block.

Ian suddenly lost consciousness and fell asleep for a while.

Chapter Seven: The Start of a Quest

"Is this really home?" Ian heard his mom call his name. Finally, the scene became clear after Lorry Lanterncup shove a flashlight in front of Ian's face.

"Zah," Ian exclaimed. "Well hello, welcome back to your house," Lorry's voice came. Ian awoke in his own bedroom. "What, where are my friends," Ian apprehensively said. "Oh, they are sipping hot-cocoa in the living room," Lorry replied, not concerned, "they are also waiting to watch The Nightly News at 6:00pm." "What time is it now?" "5:58," Lorry responded. Ian scrambled to the door.

But he doubled-over as an arm stretched out and he tummy-banged it. "Not so fast, watch your step." "Agh," Ian burbled, and he shoved the door aside.

"Hi, hi, hi." Already three greetings, and Ian hadn't even talked back in a good way, like a gentleman.

Ian turned his head, almost falling backwards and crunching up a whole bowl of popcorn with his newly-fixed back. "Whoa," Drake said, "watch it."

"Take a seat," Alexis urged. "Where's Joe?"
"Bathroom," Joe said brightly, walking out of the little room without flicking on the fan after going number two.

"Ok, let me make myself clear," Lorry started, "I am sending you all on a quest. But first, you guys need to know." "Know what," Ian cried angrily. He had enough of listening to his mom. "Shush," Lorry hushed.

"Seven thousand years ago, a phantom known as The Haunter rose to prominence and power. He created two body guards named The Shocker and The Breaker," Lorry spoke.

"Yeah, we just met the first one. He was their principal and my boss for two and a half years!" Joe groaned.

"Oh yeah, that meant I guessed right," Lorry cheerfully said, "back to the lesson."

"The Haunter used his two servants to do his deeds. Together, they possessed all the dragons. But after 5000 years, Ian's 20 greats grandfather Clive, actually changed one of those dragon's minds to doing good deeds of benefiting the future for mankind." Lorry continued.

"There was a backfiring battle where Clive found a chunk of crystal out of the Mountain of Day and Night. It made his' and all the other dragons disappear, never to be seen again."

"That was bad, right?" Alexis asked. Lorry ignored her.

"Since the dragons got extinct, Clive hid the crystal before facing The Haunter on that same mountain's summit." "Then," Drake breathtakingly asked. "Then, Clive kind of took The Haunter out of his limits and scared him off. I don't precisely know how, but the enemy retreated the next day at dawn," Lorry said.

"So, since our ancestry's name is Lanterncup, I dub the lost thing The Crystal of Len. This shall be the title of your quest. Time is precious, so start tomorrow right after you see the first hint of sunrise," Lorry said.

"You are sending us on this treacherous journey?" Joe protested. "Oh yes, and you, Joe Bark, is the chaperone."

"I have a question," Drake's hand rose, "why do we need this piece of heavy cake?"

"Number one, it is expensive. Number two, it is fragile. Number three, it is shiny. And number four, it can restore peace with a cryptic race named Shadow Clan." "Oh, I see."

"Now, I want you all to have some cookies and then go to bed," Lorry ordered kindly.

"One more thing, are we flying?" Ian asked. "No, because after a plane went missing during the winter of this year, officials have closed the airline company of our continent for what they say would be some time," Lorry answered.

Chapter Eight: A Rough Start

Morning came, and Ian was already up. Not woken up, but worried up. He thought of what his mom had said yesterday about them having to go on a quest, and also about Clive, Ian's 20 great grandfather.

There was a knock, and Ian was startled to see Alexis and Joe at the door. Ian wasn't wearing any top, so they looked away at first glance. "Put on a shirt, boy," Joe said sickly. "All right, all right, all right."

Ian got dressed and headed downstairs. He smelled oatmeal with bacon curled up on it, his favorite. Ian skipped gracefully down the steps, almost slipping and landing at split position. What is wrong with me, he thought.

"Good morning," Drake tossed a newspaper to Ian. "We missed The Nightly News at 6:00 yesterday, so I got this from the gas station."

"Please tell me you didn't borrow my roller skates," Ian begged. "I simply walked," Drake responded. "Good."

Ian sat down on his favorite chair at the usual diamond-shaped table in the kitchen. His family read the newspaper's company: The Yartian Times. They would buy a pack every week.

Ian read the title of the main article on the first page: Chain of Cars Chase through Expressway. There was a picture taken by a pedestrian of Joe with his mouth wide open and driving his car. Apparently, the picture had gone viral because Ian heard that on the radio and the TV at the same time. What a coincidence!

Ian took a bite of his bacon dipped into the oatmeal. It was so refreshing. It was just wakeful enough to beat coffee.

"People, come on, the cab is here," Lorry Lanterncup yelled. Alexis and Joe appeared at the doorway of the dining room and hurriedly hauled a couple duffel bags filled with water bottles, sleeping bags, and a few roasted turkey, lettuce, and mayonnaise sandwiches.

Drake and Ian both got up hastily and knocked over their chairs. "What is going on," came the voice of angry Lorry. "Nothing, just...just carelessness," Ian shouted back. Judging from the unusual silence, Ian knew his mother was satisfied.

As Ian and Drake approached the cab, Lorry turned Ian around to face her. "Now...The Haunter will do anything to stop you from getting that crystal, so beware. If you die, I will give you a proper funeral with teddy bears and warm chocolate on your grave. "What?" Ian cried. She ignored him. But most of all," Lorry cut short and started sobbing, "I will miss you."

She kissed Ian on the forehead and hugged him. "Uh, mom, can you let go of me now." Lorry let go.

"Well farewell, Ian's mom," said Drake, who had already climbed into the cab. "I will take good care of him," Joe noted. "Yes, bye," Lorry cried, as the cab accelerated through the countryside.

On the way to Forest Riverside Park, Ian and his friends played thumb war. Three quarters of the time Joe won.

Alexis won the remaining quarter of the time. How? She could pretty much anticipate your move and get it right a whole lot.

Finally, about half an hour later, the first oak tree came into view. "They are beautiful," Alexis exclaimed.

The cab pulled into the pick-up and drop-off zone where Joe thanked the driver and asked him why he picked the color purple for his car.

The driver explained how it meant royalty and that his dream was to be famous mechanic engineer one day. So much for a man you looked as if he never trimmed his beard for a year.

Drake started walking towards the visitor center for information. "Drake! We don't need information. A compass is all we need right now," Alexis grabbed his arm. "But I wanted a Popsicle, one of those firecracker-shaped." "NO!" Alexis answered sternly.

Joe took out a map of the forest from his shirt pocket and unfolded it. "I don't see any walkways, so use your senses," Joe said. "But I have a stuffy nose," Ian protested.

During the long winter in January, Ian had earned and deserved the cold by not wearing even a sweatshirt while playing snowball fights. It had been with him for months.

"Why are you such a pain in my neck," Joe screamed. Ian quickly made a surrender gesture.

You might think why there were not any pathways. It is because the government did not want to spend money for what the senators called "Not Relevant."

Drake lead the way as Joe volunteered to take the back. Ian ended up second in line.

Together they marched like professional hikers. Giant trees hovered above them, casting shadows.

One time, Ian thought he saw a pig the size of a bicycle. Another time, Alexis said that she heard bushes tremble. "It's natural," Drake shouted. "No, I saw it in the corner of my eye, it was definitely not the wind," Alexis claimed.

At last, they made it into a clearing with a cliff at the edge. The Kiffe River dropped into a lake the size of San Jose, creating a waterfall.

"It's so humid," Joe complained, "I wish I had ice powers to change the weather." "Well too bad," Drake replied.

Then, quicker than the human eye could process, a man in a green vest with goggles on, flew out of the canopy and taking Ian's right shoulder, flung a sword across his neck.

Drake and Joe activated their weapons, but dropped them after the man hissed at them.

"Who are you creatures," Joe yelled. The lead one answered, "We are Zartees, servants of Zark, and followers of The Breaker." He said it

48

like a desolated serpent, looking into space with his glowing-red eyes.

The Zartee on the left whispered in the lead's ear, and he nodded agreement. "We shall kill him first in a brutal way!" Every Zartee in the clearing shook their fists and shouted in a mysterious language.

"No," Ian cried. "Not Drake!" The lead Zartee brandished and pointed a revolver at Drake, who was too stunned to move. "As you know, my name is Zhowltagook." "Sure," Ian shrieked.

Zhowltagook's finger went to the trigger, Drake shut his eyes. Ian looked at him, a tear trickling down his throat.

SHIINK! SHINK! SHINK! Zhowltagook turned his head around just to see half of his men was already down.

A cloudy figure kicked Zhowltagook, who was still distracted, in the back, making his body lurch up in a crescent.

He released Ian and went rolling of the cliff, maybe was his plan of escape.

"No! We can't lose him," Joe and Alexis cried. Ian pelted to the edge, only to trip over a rock the size of a tennis ball.

"Ah!" Alexis grabbed his foot, followed by Drake, who grabbed onto Alexis' other foot, and Joe, held onto Drake's shirt, which was on the point of ripping.

"Hey," Ian called, still upside down, "help me up!" Everyone pulled, gathering strength.

They promptly collapsed when they got back on the grass. Ian took deep breaths.

Suddenly, there was a movement which Ian caught with his eye.

He pushed himself up and activated his Wrist Striker.

"Show yourself!" Ian stuttered. Out came a voice that said gently and seriously, "Hello, I am Flix of Shadow Clan."

Chapter Nine: The Weird Inhabitants

Flix resembled an armor-plated monkey. He was skinny and had white dots as eyes. Flix looked like he was powered with Neon. Blue lines traced through the outer edge of his clavicle and down the middle of his arms where they ended at six separate circles on his hands, which looked robotic. Another set of blue lines shot parallel down his flat belly. Horizontal lines (also blue) wrapped around his wrists, ankles, throat, and waist, creating belts of crosses.

What was kind of scary to Ian, was the tail. Three hands with four fingers on each seemed squeezed at the end of Flix's tail, looking like an entire hand with twelve fingers.

"Who do you work for, what do you want?" Ian demanded the truth. Flix replied sweetly, "No one."

"Then, what are you," Drake inquired rudely. "I just introduced myself," Flix answered, "here, Shadow Clan." "Hey," Alexis the smarty interrupted, "Lorry, Ian's mom, mentioned about this whatever group, I mean race." "Oh yeah," Joe recalled.

"Exactly," Flix said, "here's my story."

"We, Shadow Clan, have once ruled the planet before mankind and The Haunter. After 22000 years, The Haunter arrived from the darkness of space. By then, we were forced to exile most of the west as we were chased and hunted down," Flix summarized.

"After 4000 years, when mankind started improving their technology, both my race and The Haunter's minions became nervous and apprehensive. So Shadow Clan relocated to the far-east continent of the world," Flix spoke.

"The Haunter was not happy about mankind salvaging his property, so he gathered his forces and terrorized them. But all we did was vowed to only attack humans who dared to settle on our land at the far-east. That's my story."

"Dude, can I try out your helmet?" Drake asked. "No," Alexis interrupted, "can't you see its part of him?" "Oh, sorry."

"Well, we should camp here for the night," Joe suggested, and Ian approved. He was starting to get really tired.

"What if more Zartees come back, tracking us down, and bringing ten times they had," Alexis cried. "Don't worry, we Shadow Clan don't have to sleep, I will take watch," Flix said. "Yeah," Ian exclaimed.

The sun's ray shot through the net of Ian's personal tent, waking him and blinding his sight for a moment. He crawled to the entrance flaps and peeked out.

In a second, Flix had touched two escaping Zartees and whisked them away into the shadows.

Ian quickly put on his lace-less shoes and ran toward Flix. "Hey Flix, that was awesome!" Ian had barely enough time to pronounce the last syllable before Alexis pulled him aside into her tent.

"Hey!" "No, Ian, you can't just assume that Flix and his so-called Shadow Clan is harmless. Can you please keep a distance?" "Ok," Ian responded.

Ian stepped out of the tent, slamming into Joe, and hitting Flix's metal body with the back of his head. The last thing he saw were a pair of white dots looking down at him.

Ian awoke as Drake patted his back. "What-where?" "On the bus." "Des-destination?" "Mooda, the city." Ian looked around. "Where's Flix?" "In the shadows." "Oh," Ian understood because if typical humans saw him, they would freak out. "Why do I keep passing out?" he muttered to himself.

Five minutes later, the bus parked in a narrow lot at the Moods Land-Transporting Station. Everyone stood and was instantly relieved to.

Outside, Alexis suggested they should go to the famous pottery store of Mooda to kill time before another bus ride to Tapwa. It was about a two and a quarter mile walk, according to the map. "Fine," Ian and Drake groaned at the same time. "I need to burn some calories," Joe exclaimed.

As they walked, Ian tried to read the countenance of every citizen walking by. They looked very lethargic and haggard, he thought.

The skyscrapers were all made of either brick or wood. The buildings had no windows. There were almost no traffic at all on the streets. Few people were soliciting. Ian guessed the citizens hid in their homes most of the time.

When they got there, the store was deserted except for a couple and a bored cashier who did not even look up at them while reading his magazine.

Expensive pottery up to $1000 were on sale. Items from bowls and plates, to jugs and jars. The artwork was amazing. There were paintings from every region.

They were supposed to be a group moving around, but instead, they scattered, each one of them becoming independent.

The place wasn't that big, it was like one of those usual stores in cities, adjacent to other businesses.

Magnificent lightbulbs the size of wheels twisted into trucks hung to the ceiling with hooks. They were dangerously careening, but Ian didn't care.

Ian browsed, but he wasn't allowed to put his hands on different handworks because of ridiculous signs that read: People UNDER 16, cannot touch!!!

Of course, Ian was only thirteen, and he knew his friends Drake and Alexis couldn't too. But Joe could, he thought.

Ian then spied a glass ornament that had his three favorite colors on it. Yellow, brown, and turquoise.

Temptation swelled into his body. I have to touch and hold it, he thought. But the other half rebelled. NO! Don't be a bad boy.

Finally, as Ian was about to burst, the temptation- supporting side won.

He moved forward toward the ornament on the shelf, not even looking back, or stopping to confirm his decision.

Ian scooped it up, it was so freezing cold that Ian trembled like a 3.0 earthquake.

As he held it, the brittle item slipped between Ian's hands. Ca-Crink! No, No, No. He had to get out of there before a store salesman found out.

But it was too late, a portable surveillance camera pointed clearly at Ian and the shards of cracked glass on the floor.

Ian hastily read the tag. The price was: 689.00. There was this international law that if you accidently or purposely broke objects over 470.00, a year's jail imprisonment could be an option.

Over the shelves, voices erupted. Ian ran the way he came from. He steadied himself every few blocks.

When at last the front door got into view, Ian jogged the last row of shelves. Why was the cashier's seat empty? He thought, as it seemed as if the clerk had went to the back to check out the commotion. Then he heard Alexis' cry and Drake's struggling voice.

Ian heard a rustling sound, and he was tackled like a football player to the ground. He was so confounded that it took him several seconds to realize there was a knife's tip touching his chest.

The attacker was a man with gray hair. He looked as if he spent his entire life wandering alone.

"Who are you," Ian asked breathlessly. "Everyone shall call me, Ziknio." Ian nudged his neck with his chin.

"You really think you can make me do what you want?" Ian spoke slowly. "No! Do not ever contradict me! You, Ian, should respect me in every aspect of life," the gray-haired man replied.

"How do you know my name?" Ian questioned. "Your ancestry, counting first names, is famous in The Haunter's realm," Ziknio explained.

"It is because of what your 20-great grandfather did almost made The Haunter lose his grip on the world," he added. Ziknio pressed the dagger's cusp deeper into Ian's chest by a centimeter. Ian shuddered uncomfortably.

"So, can you tell me your story, everyone I meet seems to have a story to tell," Ian asked, as Alexis stumbled into the row, her hair obscuring her face. Someone with orange-dyed hair gripped her shirt.

"Oh yes, I will right now. Mooda was once a city for people with depression to come. It was the only place crazy people were truly accepted," Ziknio blurted vigorously.

"Over 10000 years had passed, and each generation keeps on getting more and more humorless and always sleepy and selfish."

"So, when The Haunter had dove into this planet, he made an oath to restore happiness to us. We took it, obviously," Ziknio concluded.

"Please Ziknio," Ian trembled, "I know you have developed a crotchety and acrimonious personality because of your past, but in fact, taking The Haunter's oath is by far the worst thing the Moods can accept."

Ziknio sneered at Ian, his fury increasing. "Let me tell you more about life when I was in my mid-20s."

Ian clenched his teeth and nodded, hoping it was the best way to listen to a not-so-entertaining story about a bone-showing-wrinkled-fingered old man's past to give whoever (he didn't know if Joe or Drake was still not abducted) more time to search for at least himself and Alexis.

There was a flash from a double-sword of a bow thing, and Alexis' capturer collapsed. Ziknio became aware of what just happened and smiled. "It's too late for him to save you," Ziknio chuckled. He raised the dagger, but Alexis kicked Ziknio's hand, and the dagger went skittering away. Ziknio looked up, and Alexis slapped his face.

Ziknio turned around and ran, only to get sucked into Flix's purple and green tornado-like thing.

"Yay for Flix," Drake exclaimed. Ian was sprawled on the floor, his vision blurring. "Drake," Alexis screamed, "Ian had been injected with poison!" "I'm here," Joe jumped out. "Do something!" Alexis and Drake cried. That was all Ian heard.

Chapter Ten: The Discovery of a Mysterious Island

He thought he saw glimpses of crowds chasing after him, the bus taking off, an ambulance, and the inside of an airport. It seemed to be only seconds until he shuddered and his eyes flew open.

"Steady, steady," Joe cupped his hands on Ian's shoulders. "Alexis? Drake? Flix?" Ian questioned. "NO! Just relax," Joe said as Ian scrambled up. "Then, tell me where are they!" Ian cried.

Ian looked down, and realized an I.V. line connected from his forearm to a plastic bag hanged on a pole with wheels. He was lying on a hospital bed and was wearing patient clothes!

Ian observed his surrounding and shrieked. He and Joe were in the luggage's storage under the passenger seats.

"Where is this plane taking us?" Ian asked demandingly. "Kael, where we will take a train through Roost, and to the Mountain of Day and Night."

"I thought the airline company was shut down," Ian considered. Joe replied, "Tapwa was the only place it did not." "I still don't get it."

"Fine, do you recall the time a candidate from Tapwa won the Games of Da Best? They weren't rewarded, so when the airline system closed, Tapwa's leader demanded the prize to be cheap airline tickets that won't expire. And, that its airports open forever no matter what."

"Oh, now I see," Ian answered. "So, now may you tell me….WHERE ARE ALEXIS AND DRAKE AND FLIX" "Chill boy," Joe begged.

"Tell me….right now!" Ian snared at him. "Ok," Joe started backwards, "Flix is checking out the gears in the cockpit, Drake is obviously stalking airline attendants, and Alexis said she needed a little bit of time to herself."

Ian pondered. It made sense that Flix would check out gears and Drake would stalk certain people, but why would Alexis want time for herself? To ponder? Then, to ponder about what? Ian thought.

"Hey Joe, why did the workers let us onto the plane if I was poisoned?" Ian wondered. "Alexis did everything she could to make them let you on," Joe responded smoothly. "Like?" "She

61

gave an eight-minute long speech, she persuaded them." "Alexis did that for me? She stood up for me? She was my advocate?" "Yes," Joe said.

Just then, the airplane shifted and then went down and up a series of time.

A lady's voice reverberated out of the little speaker Joe had cuddled in his hands. "We are experiencing a period of turbulence, so stay in your seats and keep your seatbelts strapped on, please. On the other hand, Mr. Voulcaner has just informed me that the plane is having technical difficulties. We are deeply sorry for any lateness. There will be refunds made, shortly."

"Can I please have this thorny-thing out of my flesh now?" Ian cried adamantly. "Well, since there is no doctor on board, I shall do it," Joe offered. "No, No, NO!" Ian screamed like a kid scared of the dark. "You can trust me, stay put."

Ian gasped with two very fat tears sliding down his cheeks as Joe removed the needle. He actually felt better, but his arm still felt numb.

The plane slowly dropped.

"Joe! Can we go to the top now?" Ian asked uncomfortably. "It is kind of dark here," Ian added. "Oh, you are afraid of the dark?" Joe teased. "No," Ian sighed.

"Well, come on," Joe stood up and walked over to a hatch with a string hanging loosely. Ian supported himself up with his good hand. He hobbled over to Joe as he pulled.

Sunlight bursts into the luggage department and Ian suddenly wished he had sunglasses.

"What time of the day is it now?" Ian questioned. Joe looked at his water-proof glowing watch. "Three p.m." "Are you kidding me?" "I never lie, kid." "I don't believe....aha, you are lying again!" Joe waved him away.

Ian hurried up the ladder, almost falling backwards into Joe's face. Ian then realized he was in one of those compartments where they kept food, drinks, tape, and all sorts of material they would most likely need.

There was a flight attendant right next to the trapdoor, and she screamed like a rooster.

After fifteen seconds, as she calmed down, a male attendant holding a pocket knife cried and jumped into the compartment, his face looking deadly.

His eyes quickly detracted from the bridge of his nose and he abruptly made a goofy smile.

"I thought there were some terrorists on board that were attempting to ambush my girlfriend here," the guy said.

"As you know, I am proposing to her next month!" "That's, great." Ian made a fake grin and gave a thumbs-up. "I hope you two have an excellent wedding!" "We will, right Tom?" The lady assumed. "Uh, Jane, you can't tell the future," Tom responded seriously.

Joe dragged Ian away around the corner, and he spoke, "That was a waste of time." "Well, not really, at least we got to know about their lives," Ian noted brightly.

Ian spotted an empty row and hobbled towards it. He went to the window seat and finally saw the environment and atmosphere outside for the first time in a 17-hour period.

Ian almost banged his head on the low ceiling as someone tapped his shoulder. He turned around and realized it was Drake.

"Please, we must take a seat," Drake ordered strictly. Ian sat and he knew Drake was about to have a conversation with him. Ian also knew he was about to be apprised.

"So....Flix told me though his shatter-proof phones that as he was checking the gears out, one kind of stopped circling. He is worried that they all would, but he says we shouldn't be too concerned about it. So I knocked on the pilot's little control panel room and I told him about it. He said it would be ok because we are halfway to Kael, and if we must, land on this remote island that does not seem to have a history. He also mentioned about calling for help."

"What if there is no signal?" Ian considered. "Oh yeah, I forget, he told me that we would have to play survival by building a few row boats of wood to get back."

"What if the waves get too strong?" "Well, I don't know, but there is no need to feel apprehensive," Drake finished.

Suddenly, the plane lurched forcefully, and Drake was thrown across the floor. Ian glided up and was thrown several rows of seats.

It was only a couple seconds to recover unto Ian limped into the aisle and saw a humungous and massive creature's head slam the left wing of the plane. Chips fell off and went flying in the air as the creature got hold of the tail and tore it off with its dirt-filled talons.

Ian saw Alexis exit the lavatory in front of him as the plane lurched backwards. Ian dove toward the opening at the back of the plane. He managed to hook on to a seat with his left arm and thankfully caught Alexis who was screaming mercifully with his right. She hanged loosely, four feet from the enormous gaping hole.

The plane then lurched frontwards and it headed straight towards the creature's diamond-hard carapace. As it descended midway, the creature tore the cockpit off. He slammed the plane again, letting it spin in 360s.

Over the unrest, Ian took glimpses through the openings on both ends. There was a sea monster that looked like a snail and a camel combined. Ian rocked his brain as he held onto Alexis' hand. He had learned it somewhere.

Aha! It was called The Snamel. Half snail, half camel, he thought. Why camel? Because there was this canyon that occupied most of the creature's back. Why snail? Because the underside was slimy and had an odor that could make a person go into a coma for weeks.

Then he thought, where were Drake, Joe, and Flix? He had to find them no matter what. But could he defy gravity with Alexis at her trust and in her own dignity?

Most of the passengers had already plunged and fell to their deaths or maybe even gotten swallowed by The Snamel.

There was so much going on, Ian thought. His brain was sick and about to explode like an atom bomb would. They were still spinning at like 200mph.

He couldn't focus. It hurt his eyes. Ian kept drifting off and awaking again. What was wrong with himself? He always thought of that.

What was wrong with himself…Nothing! Ian suddenly blinked all the confusion from his mind.

Ian carefully lifted Alexis with one hand and put her on a seat where he told her to strap on the seatbelt of the chair for just a moment.

His eyes averted to where his Wrist Striker was, attached to his arm. Ian clicked a random button which he felt would save himself and his friends out of this situation. Ian was really not always good at making decisions, especially when it was a tough life-or-death time like this.

What was the result of that button really surprised Ian. An energy ball sparkled to life in Ian's palm. What was he supposed to do with it?

Just then, Flix materialized out of the shadows and put his palm on Ian's energy globe-like thing.

All the electricity disappeared. "Ian, tell everyone still alive to assemble here, huddle up, and then the bubble shall expand and take you guys calmly to the city of Tad," Flix said. "Also, don't worry if it would pop." "It shall transport directly."

Ian made his loudest voice, barely audible over the sound of howling wind and roaring from The Snamel. "GET OVER HERE, EVERYONE STILL ABOARD AND AWAKE!!!" Ian used all the breath from his lungs.

Drake and Joe appeared, thank god, but someone else also hopped out into the aisle. It was this approximately three-year-old boy that had a deep-red-colored face which left marks from crying very much.

"Oh, he looks so cute," Alexis exclaimed. "Uh, where's your parents, youngling," Joe asked irrelevantly, still steadying himself. "Isn't it OBVIOUS?" Alexis got so mad she yanked the seat belt off and forgot all about an airplane that was going down rapidly.

Ian could feel the plane already had lost altitude, a couple thousand feet.

He yelled and shouted and screamed and cried to get their attention for the very last time. "DO YOU ALL WANT TO DIE? WELL, YOU KNOW, IT HURTS!"

They finally hurried to Ian, looking down at the ground and feeling remorseful. "On three, one, two, three." Nothing happened. Ian started to feel hopeless. "Try again," Drake urged, "It always works the second time." "Yeah," Joe agreed. Ian tried again hopefully.

"One, two, three," Ian cried. The globe glowed, and in the next instance, they were about 40 feet below the plane, heading northwest.

Somehow, it seemed like there was a magnetic field between the plane and the bubble for it spun directly towards them from above.

Ian started feeling sad and bad for all those onboard including Tom and Jane who died. The Haunter was truly evil and should pay a heavy price for his atrocity towards mankind. But who was this kid that now tugged at Ian's undershirt?

Ian turned around and studied the child. He had little freckles the size of termites and a whole lot of shaggy hair. Joe tried winking at the kid, but instead of nodding back, the boy gave Joe a visit with his back. Ian's mind felt like the aftermath of a typhoon, all damp and messy.

The kid started to go crazy with physical force in that little bubble floating peacefully and gracefully down. The child punched Ian in the hip, toppled over Joe, whacked Drake's posterior, and front-kicked Alexis in the stomach.

Everyone drooped and growled in pain. The kid actually looked pretty pleased with himself.

Ian was getting so spiced-up that he thrust forth his Wrist Striker and punched the unfortunate child in the cheeks. Ian had definitely put too much pressure, for there was left a bruise as a mark and evidence the size of a soccer ball.

Ian was really starting to feel acrophobic. It was drifting and surging through him.

Don't look down! Don't look down! A voice like a phantom came. The sea has been a place of wonders for millennia! But it also holds the darkest of all horrors! What you just saw there was only the simplest first taste of appetizer! The sea holds the most eye-catching, but the deadly ones still stir beneath, and they strike whenever it is most unexpected!

The voice started laughing like one that had just accomplished a mission to deceive the most faithful. There was no humor in it. But there was pride, imperiousness, bumptiousness, and most of all, maliciousness. A sort of evil that no man could fathom hung on that voice.

"Stop it!" Ian screamed. "Stop it!" Ian felt like a football that had been just touched down when until Flix gave him a little shock to wake up.

"Ahgh," Ian cried. He looked around, and with a heart-stopping split second, realized they were on an airport's runway.

Thing was, the plane they just escaped seemed as if it was clinging on to them, not letting go. It was skittering towards the control tower, and within subway's length between them, Ian and his friends were like geese ready to be squashed to bits of meat. Joe was already hauling up the surviving child onto his shoulders which Ian punched in the face angrily.

"Guys, people, we better run!" Ian screamed. In the distance, Ian saw another airplane descend. Ian made a hand-covering to block out the orange light of the setting sun and read the title painted on the plane. It said: Grars' International Cargo Transportation Incorporation. But in abbreviations.

"Come on! Let's go!" Joe cried. "Ian's right, we will be smooshed if we don't move quickly." Drake agreed. "Looks like Flix is always a step in front of us, he's in the shadows!" Alexis noted and put up on an extraordinary-like countenance.

They took off pelting toward the building of a terminal. Ian could make out tiny figures in action of running to the metro and police attempting to calm their emotions.

Running started to give Ian a lung-twisting feeling. His thighs were burning. Ian's veins seemed to have reduced its speed to transport messages like wires. It felt so crazy to be sprinting for his life away from a non-living man-made vehicle that was just sliding on the pavement ready to demolish them as soon as it got closed enough.

The plane had scraped the runway spot where they had just been a moment ago. Ian calculated the distance from Joe in the front to the base of the terminal.

Another plane was then accelerating speed threw a different runway, and Ian, Alexis, Drake, Joe, were forced to shut-down their sense of sound.

As they got about nineteen feet from the gates, a police from the control tower took out a pair of binoculars and then recognized them in plain sight. He then switched his target to the plane, which was already double the horde of frantic children and a very fat adult's distance away.

The airport police started shouting at fellow co-workers that were watching for free entertainment of the partly-on-fire airplane's chase with a group of lunatics. The cops seemed to be amused and not bored anymore. They started to even take bets on…based on their mouth movements, one million dollars. It was mad!

Ian had to save his friends once again. So he checked his Wrist Striker. There was a pair of buttons that were red, and one was already tried, the energy ball that lowered them directly to Tad. What if the other one was the opposite direction?

Up? He took the risk, keeping the hope that it was not some suicide self-destruct button Ian Lanterncup just pushed with his thumb.

Another energy ball sparkled, but Ian was afraid to touch it. Remember, there is electricity! Ian reminded himself. What if it shot out lasers? He thought. No way.

Alexis tapped him on the shoulder and Ian shook his head out from daydreaming. "The plane is now estimated twelve feet away," Alexis yelled apprehensively. "You are the only one with special uses in our team."

The word "team" echoed in Ian's mind. He was literally getting a headache. Of course, when anyone gets entangled, there is always a way to extricate yourself from it. Whether if it was an emotional or a physical situation. Ian pondered for a few precious seconds as Drake, Joe, and Alexis screamed at him from all around.

Flix materialized once again and sucked out all the electricity from the globe. Ian abruptly thanked him for caring and he spoke, "Take us to the closest five-star hotel of Tad from here." It glowed, and they were taken into thin air as the tip of the plane's right wing scraped the airport's control tower's antennae.

Chapter Eleven: Hotel Horror

The skyline of Tad shone colorfully through the night. It was supposed to be past dinner time, but Ian didn't care. He was exhausted! Ian kept yelling, "Come on! Hurry up, you slow old bubble." Eventually, the bubble seemed to feel Ian's pounding, stomps, and pinches to its rubber-like body.

So, to send a message of disliked treatment, it floated towards a mythical creature's statue standing on top of a pillar, adjacent to a skyscraper. Almost slamming into the repulsive face of a hawk/lion animal, the bubble slightly twisted and it brushed the hip of the statue.

At that point, lightning flashed, and Ian felt as if his heart hopped into his head because of a scare coming from a lifeless and ugly man-made stone carving.

They were now heading towards a little suburb south of Tad. In the distance, Ian spotted open field, about 55 acres. There was also something else: A building the shape of an anchor in the center.

"It's....its pink! The hotel is all pink!" Joe screeched. "How do you know? It's all dark, about an hour after sunset!" Ian questioned. "Well…"tis okay!" Drake interrupted. "At least there is some form of shelter under this ridiculous pouring rain," Alexis added.

Flix stepped out of the shadows in a tenth of a second and lifted the child which Ian, without double-checking his readied action, punched the kid in the face. Apparently, the child had been half asleep during the whole scene of running desperately on a runway.

He was muttering stuff about trucks and flying rams. Ian also caught a part where the awesome ram blasted the selfish pig with pineapple juice.

"Hey," Flix said, surprising the crew, "I will take him to the hotel first with Shadow-Travel, meet me at room 1376, I am sure it's vacant." With a blink of an eye, Flix disappeared along with the kid that had no name known to Ian and his friends.

"I hope he's not a threat," Drake considered. "What?! Of course not, he's just a three-year-older," Alexis opposed. "Well, you never know," Joe made his right eyebrow twitch. Ian thought of the phrase Joe just said and assumed it was a cliché (common saying) used in many cultures of their world. Alexis snorted, but remained quiet, arms crossed.

The bubble finally hit solid ground onto a mile-long driveway extending from the main highway to the grand entrance of the hotel. Thankfully, the bubble landed them harmlessly ten feet from the doors as it made a slight pop.

Ian led out a sigh of relief and pelted straight through the open doors, not even waiting for Alexis, Drake, or Joe. He fast-walked to the counter and a lady with curled-up hair assisted to him.

"May I help you?" Ian took a deep breath. "Uh, yes. A group of us, four friends; one adult, and three teens, would like a room, please," Ian asked. "Name?" the lady questioned.

"Uh, well, you see, we have been chased by bandits all afternoon, and are only best covert and benign place we found was here," Ian lied.

He crossed his fingers, hoping the lady would buy it, but unfortunately, she didn't. "No reservation, no place to stay," the lady confirmed.

"But—"Well hello, amigo." A man in a jacket with a bow-tie pinned to his chest turned the corner. He looked Italian and Spanish. Maybe a mix. Ian had no idea why the guy called him an amigo at first glance. He had a friendly smile and walked respectively. Even the woman who had been addressing Ian, sighed and instantly seemed overwhelmed.

"I heard a bit as I walked over here." He cocked his head towards the lady, and spoke, "Ruth, you can't have that kind of an attitude towards a customer like this!" Ruth hesitantly peered at the ground, guilt-full. "Oh well, I will cheer her up," the manager said.

He fished up a plastic card and dropped it into Ian's cupped hands. "Have a nice stay!" "I will," Ian responded joyfully.

Drake, Alexis, and Joe sat against the wall next to the elevators like hobos, begging for money in a luxury hotel.

"Guys! I actually got the card!" Joe was the only one who reacted by nodding his head. There wasn't really much enthusiasm in the squad. Drake and Alexis' eyes were heavily drooping.

The green light flashed on the door of room 1376. Drake and Alexis hobbled into the room like zombies. Apparently, the room only had a single king-sized bed fit for two grown adults.

Drake groaned at the sight of the bed. Alexis literally hopped and stomped with an angry expression. Joe just put a hand to his forehead and shook his head. And Ian, pretty much nothing.

Flix was standing near the desk table, dumping the still-asleep child onto the soft and comfy blankets.

Ian's friends started claiming personal spaces for the night. "I call the couch," Alexis cried. "Ok, then I call the table top," Drake called. "I want the bottom, then," Joe said. Well, Ian thought, I have the bathtub.

Not even caring to change clothes, shower, or even brush his teeth, Ian went to the bathroom and took a stack of towels as substitutes for pillows. Ian knew he had to be flexible in these unusual times.

✳ ✳ ✳

Water sprayed out of the shower faucet as Ian woke abruptly. His clothes were soaked. Ian hopped out the tub but slipped and fell sideways.

Joe and Drake laughed hysterically while turning off the water. Alexis pounded on the locked door, screaming for it to open.

So, it was all a hilarious little antic, Ian thought. Ian got up on all fours, and with the help of the toilet, pushed himself up. "What a ludicrous artifice!" Ian chuckled, joining in.

Suddenly, there was a knock. "Who is it, Alexis?" Joe asked haggardly. Apparently, that act of knocking had spoiled Joe and Drake's entertainment. "Some—Zah!" There was a loud BANG, and Alexis' voice ceased.

Ian flew at the door, going SPLAT! He looked up, seeing the shape of an oval getting drawn with sulfurous material that could melt down just about anything.

In an instant, an oval-shaped piece of wood the size of Drake went collapsing onto the marble floor. Joe acted too quickly.

He attempted to dive through the opening, but obviously got stuck at waist length. Joe had never really had that big of a tummy, but his waist, it was large. That didn't quite of make sense, Ian thought. How could his waist seem so big when his stomach was a tad smaller than his liver? Anyway, he was really stuck.

Joe's legs waved randomly at different items on the sink's platform. Shampoo bottles and soap boars that once occupied the little shelf adjacent to both the wall and the counter, spilled rapidly onto the floor. Some conditioner bottles' caps even popped open, creating a flood of olive-oil-like substance.

Drake tried frantically to pull Joe back into the bathroom as Ian checked if he was bleeding. Instead, as Drake kneeled to generate strength, Joe forcefully toe-tapped him in the chin. Drake rolled back, clutching his wound.

Ian knew he had to do something. Ian took a deep breath and twisted the knob. He shoved it fashionably and carefully, hoping the raider would creep out and forfeit. It was a darn low chance in percentage.

What Ian discovered was the most muscular dude in the entire universe you could fine. He had a salty scent in his hair and a cruel facial expression.

This couldn't be a monster, Ian thought, he looked precisely like an average human but with biceps and triceps the size of college dictionaries. Yup, this guy definitely could have strangled him and knocked him out like a rodent who was desperate for a place to hide.

"Who are you," Ian tried glaring at his face, but eye liquid started building up. Ian wiped his eyes and rubbed them for quite some time.

The dude finally answered, "I am The Breaker." Ian jumped back, stunned. "Some humanoid creature mentioned your name, uh, Zhowltagook?" Ian trembled from head to toe. The Breaker narrowed his eyes, not even facing Ian.

"We are favored by The Haunter and will continue to be so after you are eliminated." "Huh?" The Breaker stomped to Ian and snatched up his arms.

"One more time," The Breaker cleared his throat, "the Zartees, Zhowltagook's army, is also under me. The Haunter, he favors us the most, not counting the Dark Elves. "The what?"

"Never you mind, you are about to be eradicated. Why then are you anxious to know? You are about to perish!" Ian tried scratching The Breaker's legs with his toenails, but goodness, they were like blocks of obsidian.

"Well," The Breaker sighed, "it looks like I have to kill you by orders from The Haunter." His hand went to his trousers and magically a spike-less mace appeared in The Breaker's giant and calloused left hand. "Ugh, I hate to kill you like

82

this, I would have enjoyed several rounds of slow kickboxing where the sixth will be the death-match."

The Breaker lifted his copper mace with no effort as Ian's fear grew. The stress was too much in waiting for the strike. He felt like pinned to the wall with no freedom of movement. How could he beat this guy single-handedly?

Drake saved him. There was a flash of iron. The Breaker dropped his mace and howled. Ian dove out of the way as The Breaker slammed into the wall. Ian saw a cut the length of a pencil on his lower back.

Joe hobbled over to Ian, patting his hip to make sure it was still in a distinct shape. Alexis lifted herself up cautiously next to the curtains and walked towards Drake, eyeing The Breaker with a no-good look. He sat on the not-so-fluffy carpet like an overweight baby.

"So…Breaker, have you learned your lesson?" Ian asked. The Breaker tried to bite at his calf, but he dodged. "You're too slow!" Joe derided. Drake started to laugh hysterically again.

The Breaker started inhaling and exhaling rapidly, speed picking up. He began to have a sinister countenance. The Breaker smirked and seemingly bounced up.

"No one condescends me!" The Breaker roared with a fearsome pound on his chest with his fist.

He turned to Drake and brandished a javelin. "You shall feel the point of this…this thing first because you deserve it!!"

The Breaker threw it at him. Drake swerved away and the javelin went straight into the TV screen. Half of it was still visible.

The Breaker went at the TV and drew a diagonal line adamantly on the screen as he struggled to pull the javelin out.

"Hurry, there is not much time until he gets the weapon out. Everyone, we need to get out of here!" Alexis cried vigorously. Ian and his friends ran for the blasted-open door.

"Argh!" The Breaker finally yanked free his weapon from the broken TV and pinned it to the ground.

He sneered. "I have no choice than to use my finale!" "Well, show us, disappoint yourself, you're going to fail!" Ian had no idea why he blurted that phrase out. "Wow, you really don't think about consequences before you talk, right?"

Ian and his friends quickly made it out of their hotel room and into the corridor, advancing towards the elevators. The Breaker, however, stepped slowly out without glancing at the ground to be aware of the bump he could have tripped on. He hobbled to the center of the hallway.

Joe was first to the elevator. He pressed frantically on the "down" button. Joe pounded on the wall, hoping it made the elevators work faster, and not even caring if he woke up tourists or people on a business trip.

The Breaker's hand went to his pocket once again, and a new mace appeared. He struck a chandelier, it swung off its hook and crashed through the window at the end of the corridor. It went into the night.

Ian thought if he should wait for the elevator, or just jump out the shattered window. He seriously didn't know.

The Breaker brandished his mace yet again and jabbed it into the floor. There was a piercing glow of light, and Ian felt the ground tremble beneath him.

One by one, he saw Alexis fall vertically through an opening in the carpet, then Drake and Joe.

It was only a split second unto Ian become aware of the crack appearing around him. He grimaced and disappeared from level 13.

It was kind of hard to describe what occurred, but here is what Ian might tell you in his observation. The foundation of each level going down from 13 had pulverized because of this fiery ball that The Breaker shot.

Ian had no idea that a buff guy could do such a thing. He watched the top of the hotel implode. The top caved in like multiple waterfalls.

Ian knew that he was culpable for the situation. Ian had made The Breaker angry. Oh man, he thought, this was definitely going to be on the Extremely-Bad News Network. Ian heard the sound of ambulances.

There was a flash of blue, he felt cold air blow right into his face and then himself being settled.

Ian felt some source of concrete under him. Is this paradise? He thought. Then, there was an electric jolt.

"Zah!" Ian loved saying that meaningless word, it revived and brightened him. He tapped himself in the temple to make sure it was no flashback.

There was no sign of Flix, so he must have went back into the shadows to stay hidden from police. Ian observed his surrounding and realized the hotel looked as if it was razed by an EF: 5 tornado. Again, Ian felt sorrowful for all those who had perished from the earth. He fell to his knees.

A cop ran to Ian and said, "You are under arrest." Ian was stunned. What had he done wrong? "Mayor Mack and his officials have already decided to put you and your gang behind bars," the cop took out a pair of handcuffs. "No!" Ian jumped up and sprinted to the wreckage, calling for his friends.

The cop ran after him and snatched out his Taser. He shouted and called for help. Three other cops went pelting towards Ian from all the remaining angles.

Ian yelled, "Alexis! Drake! Joe!" but there was no reply. Then, he felt another jolt of electricity, and he was down.

Chapter Twelve: Prison Pleasure

Ian shook, momentarily seeing nothing. All darkness. He felt lethargic and dizzy. What was this place? Ian couldn't anticipate what was in the darkness. It must be a cell, Ian concluded. Was he right?

Ian called, "Is there anyone here?" No answer. He had no idea how long he had to stay in this place. Ian was also very hungry. In jail, meal times were always the same.

Ian wondered what criminals played and did in a prison for years, or even decades. Would they play cards? Work out in their cells for hours? Think about their mistakes that occurred in the past? Were there any activities like singing choruses? Did they learn how to share? Ian wondered.

He put his head between his knees and tried to not think of his growling stomach. Ian hated having nothing to do in a tight space like this. He was starting to get claustrophobic.

Light bursts into Ian's cell and Flix appeared. "Get out," he made a come-over-here hand gesture.

Ian smiled. Flix was always there to save him. It was awesome to have a member from Shadow Clan accompanying you on a dangerous quest like this. He was a blessing to Ian and his friends.

Ian heaved and staggered up, his back hurting again. "Ouch," Ian exclaimed. "Give me a minute to stretch," Ian said.

He made a spread-eagle to warm-up his muscles and starting trudging to Flix who was on the other side of the chamber. "I want to say...." "No, thank me later," Flix stared at him. "Ar, fine," Ian responded unhappily.

Ian stepped out of his cell and found himself in a narrow underground corridor the width of a horse from one side to the other. Now Ian really was feeling claustrophobic.

"Uh, so Flix, how do we....where is Joe, Alexis, and Drake?" Ian remembered. Flix looked at him, "They are outside in the courtyard, possibly being beaten by buff guys." It felt as if the world turned upside down and lost oxygen for a split second as Ian's shock exploded inside of him. Ian had to remain calm and stealthy or else he would be busted by guards.

"Are these called lamp passages?" Ian asked, touching the wall and guessing it was made of sandstone. "Yes," Flix replied, "they were used in army bases during the 1900's." "Well, lead the way, we better go."

Flix started speed-walking, kicking dust into Ian's face. He squinted, wiping the dust off with the back of his hand like a windshield wiper. Ian ran to catch up with fast-moving Flix.

Ian sprinted as Flix acted like a tour guide. "Up ahead is the Laser Arena. The only way to disable it is to go online and hack the system. I, Flix, has already done it.

Next, on your left, is the Great Chasm of Nothingness. It too has a code one must break. I, Flix, has already done the job."

"Wow, I never knew jails were so high-standard," Ian considered. "They never taught us any facts about these places in school."

They ran up ramps and went in lines that overlapped each other when finally Ian had stepped into a trap that Flix had absentmindedly forgot to deactivate.

A boxing glove in a fist-shape went straight at Ian and punched his right set of ribs. Thank God, because no bone had cracked.

They had gotten to the foot of the stairs when that happened. Ian looked around, gasping for breath. He saw a man in uniform recognize them and put a phone to his ear, suddenly looking agitated.

The man spoke quickly and sloppily into the phone, crying for help and also, "Prisoner Ian Lanterncup and Shadow Clan citizen are attempting escape, sound the alarms, we need backup." A high-pitched G note rang and there were grunts and shouting.

"Aaack!" Ian screamed, "We need to pick-up Drake, Joe, Alexis, and fly the heck out of this tormenting campus." Flix abruptly nodded agreement.

But it was cut short by the same man who ruined their mission, now holding what looked like a semi-machine gun. "Don't move, Shadow Clan citizen, I am going to shoot you."

"Tell me, what college did you attend?" Flix asked calmly, "because what kind of cop would tell a criminal that he is about to shoot him?" "Backup! You shouldn't interrogate me, I am an officer!" "Wow, you must be one that doesn't have a wise mind!" Flix noted. "Argh! I shall tore you to pieces!" he threatened. "Well, what are you waiting for, I am right in front of you."

The officer pulled his trigger as Ian blocked out his sense of hearing. The next moment, Flix appeared behind the officer, whamming him in the back of the head. He collapsed.

Together, they hurried up the stairs where Ian shifted his anxiety away, replacing it with a dose of daydreaming about skipping onto one cloud after another. It seemed as if it was an endless staircase up to the moon even though it was only six little steps the size of bricks.

They appeared in the food court where a bunch of criminals were enjoying their spaghetti and meatballs with tomato sauce. Only a few were aware of the hustle.

"Can you Shadow-Travel a few humans at a time?" Ian questioned breathlessly as they hid behind a trash can. He remembered Flix Shadow-Travelling the stranger kid that Ian punched forcefully. He waited for a reply.

"I am sorry, I can't," Flix answered. "Why not? I don't get it." Flix replied, "I am not licensed to do so." "Huh?" "Hush!" Flix glared at Ian like he was once his own best friend and just realized he was betrayed by him.

Flix gave himself a brush on the belly with his hand. He spluttered. "I can, but my curse will be set, a permanent mark shall remain, and worst of all, my great grand-children will get belittled because of their ancestor, who helped humans escape a highly secured prison."

Ian pondered and contemplated like he usually did. If Flix saved them now, the future of Shadow Clan would end up with turmoil. It was worth too much, but on the other hand, they couldn't just barge out.

"I will do it," Flix decided. "What?! No way?! You can't assume your descendants would be okay and also help us right now. There must be another way. If I had to, I will spend my life in a building of torture, getting beaten and taking naps for years. Your descendants are extremely and vitally essential to their generation. They could make a difference."

Flix blinked. "You can't tell the future, not every Shadow Clan-born one is bitter and radical, even though a majority is. I shall take the risk, just this one time."

Ian tried clawing onto a carpet as a whirlwind formed and sucked him into the void. Ian then saw the outdoors and his friends also getting pulled in. A clasp of darkness, and then countryside.

Chapter Thirteen: A Last Delight

"I have transported you four to a wheat field twenty miles from the base of the natural wonder," Flix said. Ian observed the land, and sure enough, it was glistening with the crops.

Seeing them, Ian's stomach growled even louder, forcing him to double-over. How would he climb a steep mountain with an empty stomach? Ian needed a rest, not arrest.

"Hey Flix, do you know any restaurants nearby, cause I want to eat something better than our packed and cold sandwiches." "Yeah!" Joe interrupted. "I have heard of this bistro where they serve a whole variety of fish. It is really famous online." "Then, everyone in for it?" Drake questioned. "Oh yeah," they said.

"So....direct us, Joe," Alexis called over the wind. "Um, uh, I don't really know how to get their by foot, as I said, I only heard about it on television." Only Flix didn't groan.

It could have been a miracle, but a flyer carried by the wind flew into Joe's face. He pulled it off and glanced at it.

"Hmmm, the Farm Foggy Fatted Fish Folk's Bistro!" Joe exclaimed. "What a name," Drake made his eyebrows go up. "Tis so long," Alexis complained.

"Oh come on people, I am going to faint if we don't keep moving," Ian cried. "Yes," they agreed monotonously.

"One more thing, how far away is this remote eatery?" Alexis asked Joe. Flix responded, "Two and three fourths of a mile away." "Really?" Ian knew he was exaggerating. "Listen, please, I just need to fill up my emptiness and then I will be back to my typical self," Ian quickly stated. "K, let's go," Drake ordered.

Joe looked at his pamphlet and turned it around where there was a map of the area showing. "If my assumptions are right, we are on the far-corner, southeast of this map," Joe said. "We will make it there, Ian," Alexis assured him.

"There is a little town in which we have to pass through. The place is on the opposite end. We will need to walk several blocks to our destination. Are you good with that, Ian?" Joe looked at him cautiously. "I-I-I think!" Ian stammered. "All right, let's have a pleasant stroll and exercise," Drake concluded.

"I will wait in the shadows with the little youngster as you guys enjoy. Ian, I want you to carry this in your pocket, you have proved worthy enough to carry what I am about to hand over to you." Flix took out a miniature drone-like thing. "It is how Shadow Clan contact each other, and I want you to take care of it so you can call for an emergency anytime." With that, he torpedoed into his circling vortex.

✳ ✳ ✳

The grand restaurant worth Ian's patience had finally been reached. Ian and his friends stood at the entrance, looking up with wonder and awe.

The architecture of the building was supreme. It wasn't too modern, and it certainly wasn't too archaic. Just by looking at it, Ian felt a sense of authority and honor.

The structure itself was made entirely of stainless glass. Striped black-and-white columns surrounded the cylinder-shaped building. The top was only the overwhelming part. It had acute-angled triangles sticking up into the sky, resembling spiky hair.

"Let's go in!" Ian exclaimed desperately. "Yeah," Drake substantiated. "Fish for dinner!" "Here we go!" Ian cried, cheered up partly.

Joe took a step forward and the doors extracted, revealing grand carpeting made of green and blue silk. Pearls glittered on it, keeping the carpet attracting to the naked eye itself. The flooring looked as if it was carefully cleansed every minute with popular-brand spray fit for furniture.

They walked in, not really respecting the place because of their clothing. Jeans, sweatshirts, shade-less hats, shirts soaked with sweat. Yup, really bad.

A lady with cherry-red lipstick came up to them and asked, "How was your day so far?" She sounded like a witch wanting to know how her captives were feeling. "Good," Joe responded awkwardly. "Perfect, follow me." She had a keen accent, maybe was born in Motique. Strange thing was that she didn't ask how many people were supposed to be there with them. She just picked up a handful of long menus.

The only source of light inside were candles, three on each table. It looked like a place for daters to come and talk freely without struggle. The bistro was quieter than a library. It had paintings of nature in every season strapped to the wall.

"This restaurant is so fancy!" Alexis muttered to Ian. "Agreed!" Drake said. Apparently, he had been eavesdropping.

The lady led them up a spiral staircase into a small private room. Ian looked outside, but there nothing in sight except for the mountain, the sun, and a set of cirrus clouds. Was he hallucinating? They just trudged up a set of stairs and they were like a few 10000 feet in the air? Ian knew something was wrong.

"Hey, uh, Joe! We should go back down and ask if there is another table, don't you think?" Ian smiled, his teeth showing.

"What? Did you say….? Joe hesitated, "Oh yeah, of course, that broadcaster John Buck? Yeah, he sure has a bovine voice." Ian put his right hand to his heart and back-stepped. What was wrong with Joe? Ian didn't know. He then tried talking it through with his two best friends.

"Hey, Drake and Alexis, do you two want to head downstairs for a better spot? I am afraid of heights as you know," Ian gave his best shot. Drake answered, "Why, why, why?" He put his hands into the air and waved them back and forth, palms facing himself. Alexis answered, "Oh how I long for a sheep every day of my life. They are so fluffy! My sheep shall obtain full scholarship when it supports my back as I sleep!" Ian was shocked.

"No! No! No!" Ian screamed. "Listen to me, do I have to call a psychologist right now to you people's aids, or maybe even a psychiatrist??" They didn't seem to hear him. Only Alexis talked back again, "Ian, I thought we were going to order some fish platters." Ian unwillingly nodded his head and took a seat next to the stairs, ready to dart downstairs anytime.

Drake and Alexis swiftly took the window seats while Joe sat across from them. Ian sprang to the other table, snatched a couple chairs, and told his friends to scoot over so he could fit the chairs in. They didn't seem to mind. Were they thinking of imaginary and invisible people in those seats? Ian thought.

A waitress arrived at their little dining area. She had thick hair as tall as a wedding cake. Her coiffure was a tad like a bedhead. Anyway, she radiated no charisma.

"Hello, my name is Lady H, and I will be your server." "Yippee!" Drake seemingly intentionally cried. Lady H ignored him.

"Let's start with drinks, what would you children like?" "Bloody Mary!" Joe screamed.

"Chocolate milk!" Drake demanded. "Sugar-filled iced tea!" Alexis pointed at the waitress and drew a line in the air like a queen ordering her servant to fetch her favorite snack and bring it back in less than a minute (or else he would be executed).

"Oh right, lots of orders, you all should have looked at the prices, I changed them just now, they are somewhat high." Wait, did she say she changed the prices right at that instance?

Lady H averted her eyes and glued them into Ian's. "What about you, child, I have a hunch that your emotions are kind of baffled at this moment, what about I step away so you can have some breathing room?" Ian did not answer. "How rude! I feel deeply affronted!" And with a 180 degrees turn, she stomped away.

Ian hated hurting people's feelings whether if it was a stranger in the public he just met. He always felt a source of openness in his stomach after he didn't show good manners. Ian always had a habit of picking at the veins secluded in his hands. Ian just couldn't stop it since he was five.

Alexis, Joe, and Drake started taking menus that were piled up on the table's top. Ian didn't want to ask them to pass him a menu, so he got up, made a crescent around Joe, reached nervously over Alexis, and abruptly snatched the over-sized menu into his apple-sized hand. They didn't seem to notice.

Ian walked back to his seat and sat back down, his eyes darting from one of his friends to the other. They were acting like hypnotized people that were happy because of it. It did not make sense at all.

Ian had unintentionally lost his appetite and felt as if air was enough. He rubbed his eyes as usual as his friends joyfully skimmed through their menus.

Lady H the waitress strolled back into their private space this time with a different kind of appearance. She had an interesting coiffure. Her hair stood up like it was covered with static electricity and she wore a dress that was all black.

Her exposed arms were covered with dozens of beaded bracelets. And in the middle of Lady H's neck, a tattoo shone with clarity.

It was a picture of a raven attacking a road runner in a dark forest on a tree branch. Obviously, the raven was on the point of finishing its opponent off.

"Hello, you can pretty much see that I have changed, Ian Lanterncup," Lady H spat. Ian backed-up. "My full name shall be known as Lady Harsh, and here is why."

She waved the air in front of her, and gray mist started swirling around Ian, causing him to cough. "Now listen carefully," Lady Harsh ordered.

"I was once a noble princess who loved nature and its beauty. Men were always talking about my brightness. They had big crushes on me and often asked me out for supper." She paused to take a deep breath and continued.

"It was not into another woman stole all my glory. She had traveled from the west to find a new home." Lady Harsh sighed. "Worst of all, my father adopted her as another princess and she became my sister."

"Then one day, the fairest of all men in the villages of Wobate got engaged with her and they got married." Lady Harsh started breaking up, but she kept her anguish in.

"I got jealous, and one evening, I cornered them while they were going home privately."

"What did you do?" Ian knew it already. Lady Harsh stared at him with her beady eyes, her mouth slowly pronounced the words, "I took them down." Ian didn't have to consider what she meant.

"I left instantly, abducting a fair mare from my father's stable, careful not to be spotted by a knight, and I became a wanderer. I drank unclean water from swamps and ate lizards."

The mist dissipated and Ian wiped the sweat from his forehead. Lady Harsh took off the first bracelet in line from her arm. The bracelet transformed into a ninja star in a split second.

"Good-bye Ian Lanterncup, have a nice afterlife! Tell the underground that I should be remembered as the BB, short for Bickering Bewitcher. You shall feel no mercy!"

Ian flew down the spiral staircase, shoving out Flix's gift to him. "Flix, Flix, I need help!" There was no result to it.

Ian looked out the window and saw fast-moving tanks approach the restaurant. One fired, and Ian blacked-out once again.

Chapter Fourteen: The Trial

Ian thought he was dead since of the pitch-black darkness surrounding him. But how come I still feel the same like I was on earth? Ian thought. He felt an inexplicable weight on his foot, but miraculously was still alive.

Ian's whole body ached with pain and he wished there were pills he could take. Ian always thought being a pharmacist was cool, but he hardly knew anything at chemistry. Ian didn't even know how many pills a person under 18 and above should take.

Ian considered putting medicine on the chart of fundamental needs of the modern world. It was always very useful during outdoor activities.

Ian also wished he could develop a pill that won't damage a person's liver when consumed. He just loved experimenting. Ian hoped he, himself, could start a habit of inventing and being less lazy in times of conflict. Ian knew supporting his own city state was the right, kind, and necessary thing to do.

Ian wondered if Flix was even listening to his cry in the Shadow-talk thingy he received. The gift was pretty small for an average drone/phone. It was only the size of a spoon's head. Did it even work? Or had Flix tricked him and picked it up at the Wasteland of Hardships? Ian didn't know, obviously.

Ian felt really uncomfortable under a burden of building glass. He needed some free space. Ian was an active and lively person, not a gamer who stayed in the same spot for hours. Somehow, Ian never really liked the idea of just exercising one's thumbs and sitting cross-legged on a carpet all day. It didn't seem right to him.

His lungs inflated and deflated automatically without his own intention to. He was losing oxygen under all that rubble. Ian had to get exposed to some air before it was too late. The Breaker saving him would have been an excellent option, he thought.

Ian wondered why the tank blasted the FFFFF bistro when it was occupied with innocent people who had no idea what was coming.

There was a sudden blast of light that Ian immediately blocked with both arms and his head down.

A man in a firefighter's uniform appeared. He had a slim look and a pimple-less face. "Don't be scared, I am here to help you," the man said. He extended his arm into the gap, grasping Ian's warm hand. The man pulled as Ian pushed.

At last, Ian made it out, but it was all a dirty antic. The same man that acted nicely had strapped a handcuff to Ian's other wrist which didn't have the gadget squeezed on.

"Hey! I thought you confiscated this deadly child's weapon!" A tall man with a grim face and a double-chin strolled over. "I am not deadly!" Ian protested. "Shut up," the man who was dealing with Ian ordered. That guy turned to address his boss.

"Mayor Mack, we just couldn't get it off. It was pretty much, uh, let's see, impaled into his flesh." Mayor Mack glared at him.

"What? You dare deceive me with this excuse?" "No!" The guy begged, "Please listen to me, I never lie!" "You sure?" Mayor Mack tried reading his thoughts. "Certain and guaranteed, there are tapes as evidence that we didn't do this kid a favor," the guy gulped.

"All right then, bring them into The Ultimate Court of Tad!" Mayor Mack cried. "The schedule has changed, their trial will be at five forty-five p.m. today."

"Yes, mayor," the man responded with no expression. "I will be there to watch as my day's entertainment!" Mayor Mack added.

✳✳✳

Ian, Drake, Alexis, and Joe sat handcuffed in the trunk of a Recaptured Juveniles transporting truck. They hadn't talked to each other or had conversations since getting found and forced into a filthy and strong-stench vehicle.

In the scene of a destroyed bistro, there were many survivors getting hauled into ambulances and takin to the most nearby hospital, Ian saw. They seemed to give Ian and his friends evil-eyes. All that was just a misunderstanding, he thought.

The little compartment they were in now had zero windows and felt below freezing. Ian could hear the driver and his colleague bantering and giggling about politics and sports.

The giggling sounded very much like a little girl's, Ian thought. It really did.

As the truck went galumphing through the meadows, Alexis finally broke the silence and spoke. "Ian, I have no idea how they found us when we were so hidden." "Yeah," Joe agreed. "I mean, is there like some tracking device stuck to your body?" Drake questioned. Ian patted his legs, arms, and back like an airport security guard would at that section.

He stopped and sighed, taking out his Shadow-Talk object. "I want to ask a question for all of you, do y'all think Flix is truly on our side? Or is there some suspicion that he is a spy?" Ian looked up at them, waiting for answers. "I expect a respond from all of you," Ian added.

He gave them a period of eleven minutes' time for them to ponder. They seemed to really focus.

Ian contemplated himself and thought of benefits and odds of a Shadow Clan citizen accompanying a group of humans on such traveling by foot. Overall, Flix had saved them from many attacks.

Finally Drake spoke, "My opinion and feedback of Flix is that he is triple-very helpful and gentle." "How do you know if he's not in the shadows listening to us right now?" Joe asked. "Good consideration, we can't actually meet in private," Alexis nodded her head with an abrupt awareness of the thin air around her.

The truck suddenly bounced out of a pothole and skittered to a stop with an unpleasant sound of rubber and tar. Ian and his friends literally flew up and smacked into the opposite wall.

Ian put a hand to his face and felt the touch of a solid/liquid substance that was colored red. "I have a bloody nose!" Ian screamed.

The cop outside must have heard the cry because as daylight washed in, he had a bat pointed into the trunk. His head was shaped like a grapefruit. His forehead was obscured with his dangling hair.

"Come on, we are late by several minutes," the cop ordered swiftly. "The judge wants her schedule to not delay." "Who cares?" Alexis said rudely as she hopped off the truck's trunk.

The guard rapidly slapped her as Ian tried flinging himself at him. Unfortunately, the handcuffs bit into his exposed wrists parts and Ian fell, face-plating and damaging his nose again.

Two random policemen picked Ian up and carried him through a pair of already opened doors. Ian felt like he was a dead person in a coffin being saluted in his funeral. Ian could almost feel many eyes staring at him as he was carried awkwardly down the main aisle extending from the entrance to the judge's desk/chair.

Ian felt the guards turn a corner at the base of the judge's bench. They carelessly dumped Ian into a chair as he scrambled upright, sitting straightly by taking his spine into use so he didn't look foolish.

The judge glared at him, giving a telegraph that Ian deciphered. It was something like: Don't look at me like that! Not respectful. Ian sent back one. How am I supposed to look at you, then? She didn't pause long and started giving a brief opening from The Declaration of Independence.

"When in the Course of human events…" Alexis, who sat right next to Ian, slowly raised her trembling hand.

"Yes?" The judge unhappily inquired. "Um, how are we going to proceed without a lawyer?" The judge rolled her eyes. "Someone called Cam Grog has volunteered," the judge replied like it was obvious.

"What?! You appointed an unexperienced and no college degree person to decide our fate?" "Uh, yeah," the judge darted her eyes around the room.

"Listen...." Drake who sat opposite of Alexis, on the other side of Ian, raised his hand. "You haven't even told us your name!" The judge started to get edgy. "My-my-my name is-is Judge Jade! Everyone in the continent knows. The best choice-maker of the land, full of wisdom and..." she hesitated, "knowledge, right fellow members?" Some nodded halfheartedly, and only a tad really showed that they were supporters.

Judge Jade changed the topic. "We are here today to determine whether these juveniles and this adult get sentenced to life in prison," Judge Jade summarized.

There was a WHOOSH of air and a man appeared wearing a tunic and a wool jacket over a brown muslin shirt at the front doors. "Cam Grog reporting for duty!" he cried.

Judge Jade's jaw fell. "I thought we were assembled completely!" Cam Grog pointed at her, making his finger move from one side to the other like on an old grandfather's clock.

"Ay, you should have checked by counting." Judge Jade tried defending herself. "No! That is way too old-fashioned, in the modern times, we use devices that detect and calculate for us." Judge Jade tried explaining, but Cam Grog didn't seem convinced. He quickly shuffled to his seat in the row behind Ian.

"Okay," Judge Jade went back to looking at forms stacked on his desks. "I can see that these crazy people ran on a runway and totally blew up a five-star hotel of Tad, I say they deserve three and a half decades of jail time and tough labor for causing such destruction. The children should get severely punished for their countless crimes of murder in a split second." Judge Jade spoke smoothly.

"I also heard that a local officer has some evidence to share with us," Judge Jade added. She cocked her head toward a man that was dressed in police uniform and had multiple of badges pinned to his shoulders.

He and his partner, who was carrying a plastic bag, walked formally to the Judge's bench and handed it to her.

"What?" Judge Jade looked up at them right after she received the bag. "Is this a joke?" she started losing anger management. "Y'all kidding me, right?" Judge Jade assumed to keep her anger at bay.

The officer with the badges looked at his partner and asked, "What did you do with it?" His co-worker jumped up and made a surrender gesture. "Nothing! I put it in the back seat, and it just disappeared without the bag!" "Or worst scenario," the badge-covered man started saying. "No way, I couldn't have dropped or betrayed," he hesitated.

Then, he attempted to sprint to the main entrance but a quadruple of guards seized him and dragged him out of the court room through a side door as he screamed colorfully.

"Wow," Drake muttered. "Yup, wow," Ian agreed.

"Silence!" Judge Jade apparently eavesdropped on their tiny conversation. "I have reason to put these kids and this adult behind bars because of terrorizing are city, resulting in a lockdown for a week." She paused. "I say they are culpable, right, fellow juries?" Judge Jade craned her neck. There was much muttering.

"So," Judge Jade started once again, "do we have a verdict? Have we reached a consensus? Or is the case still controversial?" Judge Jade inquired.

"We shall now do a vote," Cam Grog suggested. "Either it is guilty, or free." He paused, waiting for everyone to get ready.

"Everyone for guilty?" A couple dozen hands flew up. Cam Grog took out a monitor and used it to count. "Everyone for freedom?" About the same amount of hands flew up into the air. The color drained from his face.

"The for-guilty team has won by one! I was hoping there would be an impasse with both sides refusing to compromise, but it looks like this is an immutable decision," Cam Grog shrieked.

He suddenly dove into the air, did a somersault, and landed on the main aisle as a new figure. Who was it? Flix of Shadow Clan.

Chapter Fifteen: G-Hook Frenzy

Attorneys screamed, bystanders hustled out the door, Judge Jade fell backwards on her chair.

"Impostor! Shadow Clan in court room, deploy all cops of Tad right now!" Mayor Mack appeared in the crowd that ran out random doors. Even policemen were afraid and ran too.

Mayor Mack cried, "Come on, where's the braveness? We can't just let Shadow Clan wipe-out our elegant city!" "Then," one of the guards called back over the commotion, "if you are testifying us, why then are you running for your life? You are such a hypocrite!"

The guard made it out of the entrance as Mayor Mack jostled anonymous people and struggled to keep up in the center of the horde of stampeding warm-blooded humans.

Flix snuck up from behind and flung an invisible net over Mayor Mack and a few juries. They got entangled and started fighting each other after Mayor Mack accidentally stepped on a woman's foot.

"Hey, fatty-pants! What was that for?" "Trust me, it was not my fault." Mayor Mack tried reasoning with her, but her face gradually became a tomato with extra ketchup added. She punched him in the neck, and he tumbled.

"Burned!" Drake exclaimed excitedly. "Oh yeah," said Joe. "Beat that, Mayor Mack!" Ian chuckled.

"Guys," Alexis interrupted, "we need to get out of here before they really summon the S.W.A.T. team." "I don't think we need more prison experiences anymore," Joe noted. "Yup," Ian replied. And they sprinted to Flix who was carefully lifting Judge Jade and settling her onto the carpet.

"Uh Flix," Ian snapped, "Why are you taking care of this lady?" Flix looked at him with his blazing white eyes. "Kindness is much more than helping," he responded with clarity. "Oh," Ian answered awkwardly.

"She just was mean, I mean very mean. A judge who has already made up her mind on sentencing us for decades? Yeah, really mean," Ian said. Flix blinked like he would in times like this. "I know, but caring is the key to friendship, a better world, and a good and well-trained heart."

Ian felt remorseful for not knowing the basics of being a caring person. It was arduous work and striving to reach such a goal to really sacrifice anything for another person whom one just met.

"Hands up!" The S.W.A.T. team had apparently arrived in what Ian thought was only a minute. "Shadow Clan citizen, back up from the lady or we will shoot this scrawny girl down," the lead one pointed a pistol at Alexis.

"Fine," Ian made a star's pose, letting them do whatever they wished to him. "Take me, not my friends. I will serve as substitute for their years. Please listen to me." Drake rebuked him. "What? No! Are you kidding me? No way, we had rather die with you in prison than leave you desolate and lonely for the rest of your life."

Ian turned and looked around at his friends. "Is that seriously true?" Joe and Drake nodded solemnly with no sarcasm, humor, or hint of joking. Alexis tilted her head and gave a slight nod. Flix mouthed the words, I will if it's our fate. "I will, Ian," Flix muttered, "I will never abandon you and your friends," Flix called a tad louder.

As the nearest officer strolled to Ian, Flix Shadow-Travelled a few yards to Drake, spoke into his ear, and flung himself at the policeman.

At the same moment, Drake shoved his glade which was strapped to his back, and pulled its string with a roped-arrow in the notch. It ascended and sank into the ceiling's marble covering.

Flix pointed his hand into the air, and magically, it parted Flix's arm and shot towards the ceiling, creating a crater right next to Drake's arrow. The fist went straight down back into the opening in Flix's wrist.

"Hey Ian," Drake said, as Flix and the officers did martial arts. "Flix says your gadget has a button that can deploy a grappling hook out of it." "Try it," Alexis urged, suddenly next to Drake. "Fine," Ian replied swiftly.

Ian looked anxiously at his plate of buttons. Ian pressed one that he guessed was right. It wasn't. The gadget went haywire, blasting the wall to chunks with bolts of fire. Ian abruptly slammed the "stop" button with his palm.

He tried yet again, going with his feeling. I should have tried testing first, Ian thought. He pressed a new one, and a spider-like metal thing popped out of the opening in the gadget, spiraled up, and clung onto Drake's roped-arrow.

"Yes!" Ian cried. "We better get going!" Drake shouted. "All right, Alexis, hitch a ride!" Ian yelled. "All right," Alexis blushed.

Ian hopped off the ground, hoping it would work. They shot toward the ceiling and Alexis started screaming. "Are we going to crash? Are we? Ah!"

Ian twisted, grabbing on to Drake and they shot out into the air like a geyser, pulling their utilities back out.

Unfortunately, they went headfirst down, crashing into a bush. Pain started throbbing in Ian's forehead, but there was no time to recover.

Ian and Drake both rolled out of the bush, pulling Alexis along. "We need to act stealthy and like a typical citizen," Drake whispered.

"How are we going to in these clothes?" Ian questioned. "Um, we can just act normal and secretly take an assortment of clothes from an outdoor casual-selling store," Drake considered. "What about security cameras?" "That....I don't know," Drake sighed.

Flix reappeared next to them with an apprehensive countenance. "Let's go, they are searching the area," Flix said. "What did you do with the officers?" Ian asked. "They are kind of passed-out right at this moment," Flix responded. "Are you sure they will be okay?" Alexis shook her head into awareness and asked. "I can't be certain and sure, but there's a good chance of no major injuries," Flix answered. "KK," Alexis uttered, not much concerned anymore.

Flix changed the subject. "What my Shadow-Map says, is that, the tree line surrounding Tad should be several blocks from here."

"I don't get it, why didn't they build the court in the heart of the city?" Drake questioned. Joe suddenly appeared behind a tree, unharmed. "Because they feared that it would be burned down in cases of angry protesters," Joe exclaimed.

"Wow, Joe, I didn't know you were that smart!" Alexis noted. "Didn't I tell you....I watch the TV for educational purposes," Joe looked at her with disbelief. "Oh yeah," Alexis called, a little shaken up.

"We better hurry," Flix interrupted softly and swiftly. "My police detector is telling me that the whole department stationed in this city has been searching for us lately. A group of fourteen is just around the corner, seventeen feet away from this thorny bush you three went dropping rapidly into." "Youch, much have hurt at some degree," Joe thought.

The first two guards appeared carrying loaded long-ranged guns with both hands at ready point. Guard one fired at Flix, missing him by an inch as he dodged into the shadows.

"Ian, Drake, use your grappling hook and roped-arrow to get from the tops of buildings to buildings," Alexis cried.

Ian acted. He pressed the same button that activated a grappling hook in any direction his gadget pointed. An iron claw shot out to the nearest structure in plain sight. A statue.

It was a guy with a somewhat large beard that connected to his hair (shaped like a hammock). He wore a traditional coat with buttons the size of bird's beaks and a very tall collar. The statue wore long pants that were too loose for him (a belt kept most of it on). His eyes looked sharp and very unchildish.

It flew at it, clinging onto its elbow and creating marks on it as it lightly scratched some of the paint off. Ian jumped off the ground for a boost, momentarily forgetting to pull Alexis along. Fear smoldered inside Ian at the sight of the hard concrete body of the statue.

Ian went straight towards the statue's lump of fat. He managed to stretch out his palm and push himself back. Ian somehow flipped backwards and kicked the statue's hip with both feet at the same time.

His grappling hook lost grip and Ian went flying back to where he started. Ian literally screamed like an alarm. He wondered when the S.W.A.T. team was going to shoot him down.

His grappling hook went twisting and drooping aimlessly. Ian knew he had to concentrate, even in midair. But he just couldn't with no training, and of course, experience.

The hook finally clung to something firm. Ian attempted his best. He urged himself to go sideways into a building and bounced off with the back of his hand. Ian went flying into The Ultimate Court of Tad. Why does it have to be this, out of so many man-made structures?

A police officer strolled serenely right in front of Ian as he went dash-flying towards the court. "Get out of the way, get out!" Ian screamed. Too late.

Ian last saw Mayor Mack hobble outside the court room. Ian then lost sight of him as he went colliding into the guard, who went crashing sideways into Mayor Mack. All three went flying towards Judge Jade, who had recovered on the opposite end. She led out a piercing cry as Mayor Mack's enormous back smooshed her into the wall.

All four collapsed, calming themselves up. Ian realized his hook held onto the lamp on the judge's bench. He tore it off with frustration swelling inside of him.

Ian wondered where his friends were. Anxiety and worry smoldered inside him. What if they were caught and put into another jail transporting truck, never to be seen again to Ian? But the other half rebelled. No way, they are simply ok with Flix's guidance.

"Up, crazy want-to-fly person! I have got whoever you are cornered with the best full-of-brawn police in Tad!" a shrill voice came. "Up! Out! To prison!"

Ian had no better choice or option. He stood, hands up. "Aha! It's you! Most wanted!" the same guy said in his S.W.A.T. team masks. "Yeah," Ian replied monotonously, "it's me. You have got me at last." The guy cocked his head. "You know, if this is another antic to escape, we are summoning the military!"

He waved his hand in front of him. "Anyway, I have got orders, but that doesn't matter. What matters is that I will get a reward for recapturing you!" The man exclaimed. "How much?" Ian asked, trembling from head to toe. "Ten-million dollars," the man cried cheerfully.

His colleague nudged him, and he turned around. "I thought you were going to split it in half!" His colleague said. "Um, I never agreed." "Yeah, you did!" They started arguing as their former co-workers tried breaking them up.

Ian slowly shuffled sideways. Now could be the moment to make his escape out of a side door. He continued shuffling down steps from the judge's bench to the floor, the S.W.A.T. team didn't seem to be aware of him.

"Hey!" One of the former members of the squad shouted. "He's slowly moving away!" "Get him now!" The lead yelled, turning his head and averting his eyes.

Ian sprinted towards the nearest side door. It was six feet away, then five. He had to make it.

There was a sharp spill of physical pain and Ian Lanterncup fell and bumped his head on hard ground.

Chapter Sixteen: Joe's Secret

Water touched his body as he shook and woke abruptly. A hand pushed him lightly back down. Who was it?

Ian blinked and looked up to see Alexis grinning down at him. What was she doing?

Alexis took a piece of canvas and dipped it into hot water in a tin-made bowl. She then cupped it onto Ian's upper part of his arm. Ian asked what happened.

"You got shot," Alexis responded smoothly. Ian's jaw fell. He, himself, was still alive? "More description," Ian begged.

Alexis cleared her throat. "As Flix took out his Shadow-Watch binoculars, Drake pointed out that he could see a body on the carpet of the court room being dragged by the S.W.A.T. team."

"Wait….where were you guys hiding?" Ian interrupted rudely. "I was getting there! It was going to be in the next sentence!" Alexis exclaimed. "Oh, sorry Alexis," Ian looked at a nearby bird who perched on a branch, tweeting. He did it to escape from the stare of her like-glowing eyes.

Alexis wasn't an irritable and foul-tempered person with much aggression, nor did she have a choleric demeanor. She was very congenial and affable. Ian loved her personality. It was mind-relieving from all the headaches and troubles of the public society. Alexis was also quick to escaping anger.

The only thing Ian detested about Alexis was how she wasn't imperturbable in fast-acting situations.

Alexis took a deep breath and tapped her fingers on the soft grass. "We were hiding behind rocks, as easy as that!" Alexis explained. She continued.

"As Flix surprised the guards and knocked them out, one by one, Drake, Joe, and I, went ducking under rows of seats, finally reaching the front. We realized it was you.

So Joe took the honors to carry you out the closest side door. Drake and I sprinted after him through the riot-caused town where citizens pelted us with stones, grocery bags, and plates. Joe got a cut. We ran for dear life." Alexis summarized.

"So....how did you three get out of that place without a helicopter spotting you?" Ian questioned. "Well, Drake told you this, I think. We formally and quietly took a few pairs of jeans, khakis, and thin typical shirts without cartoon characters on, obviously. We tried not to make a big scene and stand out," Alexis said.

"Yeah, it makes sense," Ian replied nicely, pondering. "So where are we now?" Ian asked. "The North West Woodlands," Alexis noted.

"It sounds familiar," Ian started, thinking. "Isn't this place one of the most famous national parks of Adolko, our world?" Alexis answered, "It was once one until they closed it down, never to be opened again." "Why?" Ian asked curiously.

"Sorry, I'm not in the mood to tell you." "Is it because you are from Mooda?" Ian laughed hysterically, Alexis didn't seem to find it humorous.

She got up and marched away, leaving Ian desolate. He thought about the beauty of nature surrounding him.

The flagrance of blooming flowers smelled like wet soil. It was already mid-spring, almost April. Pollen swerved through the air like feathers carried by a light breeze.

Ian's eyes started itching. His nose also started getting stuffy. I need to go inside, Ian thought. But was there an inside nearby? He doubted it.

Suddenly Joe's voice came. "Since daylight is going to last only another hour, we should camp here for the night," Joe highly suggested.

"Hey Flix! We will be happy enough if you take another all-night watch for us!" "Yeah!" Flix responded from a distance. "Make sure you don't whisk us into the shadows in our deep sleeps," Joe noted. "Ok," Flix replied.

"Hey Joe!" Drake Voulcaner's voice came, "can we have some marshmallows you brought from your rental home before curling up into our sleeping bags?" "That's is pretty darn fine with me, why did you bother to ask?" Joe questioned. "Just-just double-checking," Drake said. "Well then, set up the campfire," Joe cried excitedly. "K, I need assistants," Drake exclaimed.

Ian hopped up, doing a better Chinese Getup. "Me, me!" Ian volunteered. Drake looked at him like a homeless person with those glaring eyes and yellow teeth. "But isn't your arm still numb from the shot?" Drake asked. Ian started sensing pain in his entire arm to his shoulder blade.

"I think I can handle logs with one hand," Ian defended. "I used to lift three pound weights!"

Ian noted. Joe suddenly appeared behind Drake and they both arched their eyebrows.

"You think?" Joe answered. Drake jumped into the air and put his hand to his heart. He turned around.

"Wow Joe, that really scared the heck out of me," he said. "Next time," Joe started, "watch your own back and don't let me or Flix do it!" Joe finished. "Yeah, you're right, I should be more aware even in unusual places," Drake responded. "You call this an unusual place?" Joe questioned. "No! I didn't refer to this woodland."

"Fine, now gather the logs, we need a campfire before it's too late for one," Joe ordered. "It's never too late," Ian replied. "Oh well, we need to get better rests since these several days have gone by without even a peaceful night," Joe concluded. "Yeah," Drake corroborated. "Right then, we need firewood!" Ian cried. "To work," Drake yelled. "Excellent," Joe exclaimed.

Ian limped roughly to a pond surrounded with logs that frogs sat on. They were the sizes of long chimneys. Ian picked up one without mold or wild mushrooms growing on it. Also one that didn't have bird poop splattered on it (a majority did have).

He hauled it up, struggling to keep it on as it slowly slipped off his good arm despite of the sandpaper-like bark. Ian thought it was an easy job, but unfortunately it wasn't.

He now started realizing how much stress people with amputated limbs had to go through. The truth is: People had to experience what another claims to have in order to truly understand the fun or frustration.

A quarter of an hour later, the log-gathering was done. "Attention all members of The Crystal-Recovering Squad, get over here," Joe shouted through a pretended microphone, using a hand. "Yup, Joe said get over here right now, and that is what you are supposed to do!" Drake confirmed.

"Wait Joe, you made a name for our team?" Ian asked. "Well….Drake supported me with ideas, and I pretty much just eliminated the ones I didn't like." "Just?" Drake questioned. Joe sighed. "Okay, no," Joe answered.

Ian limped dazedly, already getting very tired and exhausted. He needed a break, not a broken arm that refused to carry things at his own will.

"How is your tied-up wound?" Alexis stepped into the clearing with an apprehensive

131

look. "Are you sure your arm is still workable? I would be happy enough to chop it down for you!" Drake asked sarcastically. Ian took a deep breath. "No-o-o way!" Drake grinned, satisfied. "Are you sure?" "Of course I am!" Ian cried joyfully. After a few seconds, "Yes, I am," Ian confirmed.

They turned their heads to the campsite Joe prepared. The campfire was set in the middle. A semi-circle of logs stayed waiting to be sat on. The tents were on the other side of the fire.

Joe wiped off dirt from his hands with a piece of wet canvas. His muscles looked toughened up. Joe in fact seemed to have gotten brawnier since the pass week of travelling. Maybe because it was his duty to watch over the kids.

"Joe! You are an expert at designing platforms!" Alexis exclaimed. "I mean, really!" Joe just waved her away. "I only went up to third grade in my entire history of education," Joe tried defending but couldn't outsmart or overtake Alexis. "No way, you must have attended a nice elementary school," she spoke once again. "I don't think so," Joe responded clearly.

"Ok," Drake interrupted, "Let's just sit and have a little chat!" "About what?" Alexis asked irrelevantly. "Anything," Drake spoke, "freedom of speech, right?" "You can also criticize or comment on how someone's doing," Ian added. "Yeah, that too," Drake quickly confirmed.

Everyone assembled. Joe passed out the marshmallows to them, one by one. Each got a fair and equal amount. Joe sat down, finally. And everyone just stared into the void with nothing to talk about.

At one point, Joe hesitated and stuttered. "What's wrong, Joe?" Drake and Ian questioned worriedly. "It's just….nothing!" Joe answered awkwardly. "Yes, it is something!" Ian cried.

Each one of them redirected their attention to Joe. Even Flix seemed curious and burst out of the shadows through his swirling tornado-like thingy. Joe suddenly had rosy cheeks.

"Tell us," Drake urged, "we don't bite and snicker." Joe sighed once again. "Its….a secret of mine's, and I don't know if I should blurt it out," Joe responded. Ian blew air, "Its ok, your choice, your decision." Joe relaxed. "Yes, I suppose I will."

"But please don't run away and hide because of what I am about to announce," Joe pleaded. "Don't worry," Ian said.

"I am not human, I am a creature named, a Gock." Ian turned his head to look at his best friends. Drake looked fine, but Alexis seemed as if she was on the point of darting several miles away in a split second. Joe ignored her and continued.

"We Gocks have special abilities like detecting poison. My kind can live fairly a long life, about 400-420 years at most. The history of Gocks weren't very interesting to humans, so they haven't added it to their curriculum in schools. When a Gock grows up, they learn to share a whole lot. That is why whenever you meet one, they are very friendly and generous." "Like you," Alexis noted. Joe smiled and uttered, "Thanks." He continued. "However, they can sometimes lose temper-management."

Joe stopped abruptly, his face bright red with a hint of purple. "Any comments?" Joe asked, putting on an investigating face. "Come on, blurt it out!" Joe cried. Drake saved Ian and Alexis from awkwardness.

"Dude! That is so awesome!" Drake whistled. "What other special powers do you have?" Drake questioned like a six-year old kid obsessed with superheroes who had just met his favorite one. "Well uh, I have telepathy and very good hearing!" Joe exclaimed, more relaxed and open. "You know, every sound wave flying straight towards us, in other words, ones that are going north now, I can actually detect them from several miles away." "That is so cool," Drake noted.

"Then…." Alexis paused, but resumed, "Why didn't you tell us in the first place, like the beginning of our quest?" Joe's grin faded. Ian and Drake groaned, not so curious anymore. "Be….because, I didn't know you guys were matured enough to not laugh hysterically at my secret," Joe answered. "Wait," Alexis started again, "Why is it a secret?" Joe became even more nervous and anxious, at least it seemed like it. He was really getting a deep purplish color.

Ian's only dislike about Alexis was how she needed an explanation for a situation or issue. It was a hundred percent annoying. Oh well, Ian thought after a little while, every girl is like that anyway.

"Let's not talk about that for now," Flix suddenly burst out of the shadows. "What we really need is a good sleep and rest, for we shall wake at dawn to march towards the Mountain of Day and Night to recover a long-lost archaic object." "Why are we going to march?" Ian asked.

"It's just an expression!" Flix replied calmly. "I thought you went to school, unlike Joe!"

Ian returned a goofy smile with his tongue sticking out. He hobbled to his already set-up tent. Ian's arm felt much better after a late-dinner of marshmallows. The meal itself wasn't really nutritious at all, but Ian still felt blessed with a personal duffel bag which he could pull food out of to enjoy anytime.

Ian pulled down the zipper and dove through the entrance flaps. He was happy for a bed he didn't have to share with at last. Ian collapsed on his inflated mattress and began snoring.

Chapter Seventeen: Hazardous Caving

Ian woke with a fresh start, feeling strange. He was still in his tent, so what was necessary about that he felt strange? Must be something going on outside that he shouldn't miss, at least it seemed like it.

Ian lifted himself to standing point (apparently, his tent was exactly the length of him). He shoved the entrance flaps aside with both hands, like a magician revealing himself right at that spot in front of a frenetic crowd.

Ian froze to see Alexis a foot away from a fox who glared at her. Ian looked around if anyone was also awake. There wasn't. He wished Flix was here, for he sometimes went to explore the terrain that surrounded them. Ian knew something had to be done. It was really risky, but it was for Alexis.

Ian went charging towards the fox, jumping into the air and landing face-first into dry mud. Now he, himself, definitely just made the fox aware of him. Ian couldn't really roll away, for a concussion suddenly occurred.

Ian came into focus, Alexis looking down at him. "How long?" "An hour! You wasted us an hour's time!" Alexis yelled adamantly. Ian stared at her, stunned. Was she exaggerating? An hour's time wasn't much.

Ian wondered why he wasn't teared apart by the fox he attempted to scare off. It wasn't really large in size, but Ian was sure it could have ripped him to pieces in seconds.

He managed to say, "What happened?" Alexis cleared her throat like she would before giving a speech. "Sit up first, if you are comfortable to," Alexis ordered. Ian scrambled up with the help of Drake's hand, which just appeared in front of his face.

"Ahem," Alexis started formally, "I discovered a power hidden inside of me," she exclaimed to Ian cheerfully. "Keep going," Ian urged. "I can actually talk to animals!" Alexis cried.

Alexis stared at him, lost in thought. Ian started to get uncomfortable, so he asked, "How did you find out?" "Oh," Alexis got back into awareness. "Remember that fox I met? As you tried scaring it off, I don't know how, but I talked to it. I told it to not hurt you, and I also got her name! It's Rook!"

"Really?" Ian nodded his head moderately several times, demanding for the truth. "Yes,"

Alexis responded, happy to find out a hidden power she had her whole life.

"Good for you then," Joe interrupted, "I am sorry to break the excitement, but we should start walking to the natural wonder." "Aren't there any taxis or buses to transport us?" Drake questioned. "No," Flix said, appearing and leaning on a tree. "My cab-check tells me that there are none that can take us to the mountain."

Ian sighed. "I guess we really do have to walk and sweat to burn some calories!" he exclaimed with not much enthusiasm. "All right, we can do it," Alexis piped, "uh Flix, how many miles is it away from here?" "Exactly nine to the base," he replied.

✳✳✳

They trudged through open and unowned fields, hunched back and taking out their water bottles at certain times. Each step felt like torture. It lasted until Drake complained.

"My duffel bag weighs tons! Can I just toss mine's into a stream and forget about it?" Drake yelled stubbornly. "Oh come on Drake, what about when we get hungry?" Alexis pointed out. "There are places called eateries!" Drake shouted. "What if our money gets lost or stolen by bandits?" Alexis glared at him. "Break it up, break it up," Joe put his hand between them.

Ian watched, not realizing he was biting his own nails for a whole minute. Ian never really did build up a habit like that.

They continue to stroll, Ian felt like a wall that divided an empire into two. It was because Alexis went to one side of Ian, and Drake walked on the other side of him. None exchanged a word to each other for another half hour.

Ian sweated like crazy. It soaked the back of his yellow shirt, making it transparent. Ian kept falling behind to avoid letting any of his friends to see it. Except Flix would just Shadow-Travel himself backwards to make sure Ian was not their tail, who had a good chance of getting abducted with none of them noticing.

Two hours past with Ian, Drake, Alexis, and Joe crumbling onto ticklish grass. Flix kept telling them not to give up. Ian was almost out of water from his bottle, he wished there was a water fountain for the very first time. He always thought of the rust growing inside its pipes.

"Hey Flix," Ian wondered, "How did we hang on to our duffel bags after running into so much trouble?" Flix chuckled in a machine-like way. "I can Shadow-Travel items, you know." "Wow," Ian exclaimed, "you are amazing!" Flix shook his head to get away the attention. "It wasn't much," he concluded.

The closer they got, the mountain seemed to approach them itself. It was the highest and tallest landmark in the world. The mountain's summit appeared at an estimated 45000 feet. Ian tried having a glimpse at one of the three peaks, but the rays of sunlight beat down on them madly, making it almost impossible. In the distance, hikers attempted to climb the snowy mountain with much concentration and confidence.

"Good news," Joe called from the front, "We are just a mile away!" Everyone celebrated by throwing their duffel bags into the air and catching them. Alexis picked up a dandelion and blew it. White pebbles fluttered through the air.

"We must not delay! We can do this!" Joe added. "How are we going to delay? We don't even have a deadline or something," Ian questioned. "It's just an expression to get you all to listen up," he replied. "Okay," Ian answered.

For the next ten minutes, Ian thought back to his cousin, Jarret, and his funeral. Ian's aunt had used up a dozen tissue boxes. They had buried him with many bouquets of Jarret's favorite kind of flowers, lilacs. But Ian had to get something straight.

Ian didn't get why the figures (he realized they were Zartees) had vaporized right after Jarret plunged. "Why?" Ian cried, a tad loud.

"Are you okay?" Alexis and Drake asked harmonically. Joe stopped abruptly and turned his head around. Flix just flexed his hands like he was bored. "Yeah," Ian responded swiftly. "I was just pondering about stuff." "Stuff? Negative or positive," Drake questioned demandingly. "Uh," Ian started.

"Hide!" Joe lunged at Ian and his two best friends, taking them down to the ground right behind a rock the size of a grand piano. Flix disappeared into the void.

"What was that for?" Drake yelled. "Shhh," Joe hushed. "Ian, didn't the leader of the police department of Tad say that if you escaped once again, they will summon the military to search the whole continent?" "Yes," Ian confirmed. "Ok, because several troops armed with assault rifles are just a few feet away from us right at this moment," Joe apprehensively whispered. "Oh man," Ian said.

"But Joe, how are we going to find the crystal in broad daylight?" Alexis asked. "Well, what if the object is in a cave?" Joe wondered. "Excellent, Joe, we can first go caving!" Alexis exclaimed, a tad soft.

"But how are we going to pass the troops?" Drake questioned, changing the subject into a sticky issue. "What about we dig?" Ian suggested brightly. "What?" they replied.

They started protesting with excuses. "I will get my brand new shoes dirty!" Alexis complained. "I have really bad, very supreme claustrophobia!" Joe cried softly. "What if we get stuck?" Drake wondered.

"Stop!" Ian cried, a tad too loud. "What was that?" the nearest troop strolled over. Ian gulped with his heart pounding anxiously against his chest, desperate to be freed.

As the troop leaned over to take a peek, Joe jabbed him in the cheek with the butt of his rifle. The guy fell backwards, dazed.

It quickly transformed into a staff as Joe hopped out of his hiding space, twirled his staff, and went charging at a group of armed corps.

One by one, Ian and his friends jumped out. "We need to cross to the other side, I see a little opening," Alexis called over the rapid gunfire. "You sure it does not lead to a cul-de-sac?" Drake shouted. "It's our only chance to survive without getting gunned down or sent back to an even higher secured prison!" Ian cried. "Let's go, come on," he urged.

"What about Joe?" Alexis asked. "No more time to talk, I adjourn this meeting," Ian concluded, "we have to hustle!"

They sprinted like llamas being chased by tigers to the other side. "Joe, Joe, get over here!" Drake yelled as they literally dove through the gap.

Joe elbowed several more soldiers in the nose and pelted to them. He made it just in time as a bullet zipped past him. The troops quickly recovered and they advanced toward Joe mainly, as least it seemed like it because of the eye contact.

Joe turned around, grinning. "I have got this," he said. Joe took his staff and jabbed it into a crack on the upper part of the wall.

The rocks below fell onto the rocks adjacent to the ground, creating a barrier like a dam. The soldiers outside started pounding on the newly-made barricade. Ian caught his breath.

They turned around and observed with awe at the wondrous beauty of a cave. It was the size of a medieval castle. Stalactites grew from the top. Stalagmites grew from the floor and rose to the ceiling. Some joined and formed a column.

A body of water glittered in front of Ian. He saw a boat made of lumber and a paddle in it floating on the water, chained to a thick column. Maybe it was Clive, his 20 great- grandfather that used it to get across.

Ian looked in the distance, seeing glowing purple light. It must be the crystal, Ian thought, as he grinned with ebullience. "We must get to it!" Ian cried.

"Hey guys, this is too easy, we just need to row that boat to over there and retrieve the crystal," Drake exclaimed. "All right then, let's board that boat!" Joe ordered.

They trudged to it, making sounds reverberate. "Ay, why is it so cold in here?" Drake complained. "Well, live with it!" Alexis glared at him. Drake did not protest.

Joe went first to where the chain met the column. Alexis also walked over to check it out. "There is a key hole," Alexis pointed out. Ian groaned. "Don't tell me we missed something," he cried. "No way," Alexis said.

Drake strolled over, investigating. "I see that there is a sort of carving in the limestone on the ground," Drake exclaimed. "What?!" Alexis hobbled over. "Yeah, didn't I tell you I took forensic science in summer camps?" Drake started bragging.

Joe took a glance at it and put his shoe on the carving. He started applying pressure on his foot. "Yes!" Joe's shoe sank several inches into the limestone. He lifted it as Ian snatched up a piece of metal. It wasn't really shaped like a key, but Ian tried with a standing-strong heart.

He inserted it and twisted left, nothing happened. Ian tried again, getting frustrated and losing hope. He twisted right, it actually worked. The chain loosened its grip and they went SMACK on the ground like whips.

Drake took hold of the boat so it wouldn't float away as Joe hopped in first, then Ian, then Alexis, and finally Drake hurtled the railing onto the back, causing a splash. "Why am I always

146

last?" Drake asked. "Not really," Alexis recalled certain times.

Alexis volunteered to paddle their way. "Make sure we don't crash," Drake warned her jokingly. "Come on, this isn't even going at least above 10mph," Alexis answered.

They sat silently, observing in-mountain nature. "Hey Joe, can we light a candle you brought for extra lighting?" Ian asked. Joe unclipped his bag (which had materialized next to him, Flix's job) and rummaged for one. "Aha," he brought out a tiny one the size of a thumb. Joe also took out a lighter and lit it. The little fire flickered.

A drop of liquid fell onto Ian's head. As fast as possible, his hand went to his hair. "Stop," Alexis ordered. "It's just rain that seeped through soft mud in the mountain." "I thought the whole inner side was solid," Drake argued. "Whatever," Alexis rolled her eyes.

The purple light glowed, forcing Ian to squint. At last, the boat hit hard ground. Ian stepped out of the boat and saw what was in front of him.

It was just a sandy platform with spikes growing out of it on either side. A crystal with a flat bottom sat waiting to be retrieved for thousands upon thousands of years. It looked like a lotus flower that was in the middle of blooming.

Ian touched it with his pointer finger, and everything started to go wrong. An earthquake erupted, and a voice spoke inside Ian's head. Leave it alone, do not take it. It repeated the phrase a few times before Ian got back to self-consciousness.

"Ian, we need to leave!" Alexis called over the erupting earthquake. Ian trembled, and suddenly a wall of stalactites fell down and landed in front of Ian like nails pinned to the ground, making him seem like behind bars.

Drake raised his glade and sliced the stalactites into halves. Ian quickly grabbed the crystal and he and Drake jumped into the boat as a wave of stalactites crumbled onto the platform where the crystal had been.

The boat careened dangerously to one side where Ian and Drake both landed. Alexis threw herself to the other side to avoid the boat from capsizing. Joe started paddling rapidly.

They helped Joe by scooping their hands into the freezing water and driving them backwards, then lifting them again for a second round. Ian and his two best friends frantically followed the same routine for a couple minutes as the mountain shook.

They finally hit hard ground. All four hopped out of the boat as a column collapsed on it, sending a shock wave.

They ran to the barrier that Joe created. Ian glanced at his Wrist Striker and pressed another random button. There was a blast of fire, and the rocks just disintegrated. Ian had no time to admire his gadget.

They sprinted into the afternoon atmosphere, but halted. Six soldiers with loaded guns created a semi-circle so they would have to beat one up to break it. "Oh yes, here they are, the VIPs!" The middle one exclaimed. "We are VIPs?" Drake inquired. "NO! It means....Very Important Prisoners." The lead one explained.

"You know, we have orders to kill you people," the soldier on the left of the lead one said cheerfully. "If court didn't even work out for you people, then sudden death is the only option," he chuckled. "Right, fellas?" They nodded. "Here we go!"

Chapter Eighteen: The Three Dragons

The ground rumbled. Enormous igneous rocks rolled rapidly down the steep edges of the mountain. Stones and minerals flew into the air and plummeted.

A long-ranged and treacherous mudslide had apparently started, causing avalanches. The mountain suddenly became vulnerable to its own element. As boulders rolled down, they left thick trails of scars.

The soldiers looked up, distracted. "Hey!" One pointed out, "Why are the peaks moving?" "Say what?" The lead troop asked. "No! I am not kidding or hallucinating. Trust me, the three peaks are really stirring and looking as if they were the heads of some kind of massive creatures."

"We better go," a shy and timid soldier part of the semi-circle said. "You're right, but what should we do with these VIPs?" The lead one asked.

"I know!" Another troop raised her hand. "We can just ditch and abandon them here so they would die on their own, consider it." "Hmm, we should first take their belongings to leave them hungry and desperate," the lead one demanded.

"And who knows, they might even end up eating poisonous mushrooms just for the sake of dear life!" he added.

Suddenly, a humungous silhouette appeared on the open land right next to the base of The Mountain of Day and Night. Ian trembled with fear smoldering inside him. He decided to take a glance up at the sky to see how the beast looked like. Judging from the silhouette, it had a thick snout and long talons that were seven times sharper than nails themselves.

The mountain's middle section looked like it was slowly being decapitated by an invisible and giant man. A beast with shards of crystals on its hide rose out of the gigantic hole. Lava overflowed and poured out of the festering gap in the planet's crust. The entire upper half seemed to have gotten engulfed by the beast.

As its tail whipped out of the mountain's lower half, Ian had no doubt that it was a dragon. He had no idea how the dragon had survived and forced to camouflage in a natural wonder over several thousands of years. Ian thought they were extinct since his ancestor, Clive, had made them all perish.

No wonder news reporters always talked about the change in height of the tallest landmark in the world. It was always one of Adolko's biggest mysteries throughout history.

Random people just gave speeches of theories they made up. Some were really ridiculous that the veins in Ian's ears always started throbbing. And sometimes, when he frantically reached for the remote control to turn the TV off, he would just knock over a large bowl of sweet kettle corn, hordes of ants just came crawling into the living room.

Ian watched both with and in horror as two more dragons rose from the other two peaks on either side of the Crystal Dragon.

While the other two struggled to climb its way out, Ian heard the Crystal Dragon speak to him in his small brain. He somehow knew it.

"You scared and fearful now? If you believe in yourself, in your own strength despite of your size, try going at me, and I shall pierce you with one of my signature and very sharp-tip spikes," it spoke. "Always remember, beware the tail, it hurts a whole lot when it even gives your thin and fleshy skin a slight scrape, or shall I say, a visit," the Crystal Dragon added.

Ian shook his head back to reality. There were now three dragons perched on the rims of their hiding spots. This time, the Crystal Dragon literally opened his mouth and spoke English. His voice boomed through the valleys.

"Hello, and welcome to The Mountain of Day and Night," the Crystal Dragon formally announced. Ian looked at the soldiers next to him, they seemed to be in shock and disbelief. "Let me continue!" A humungous microphone could have been tied around its neck, because its voice just sent shivers.

"So this is the Sun Dragon, and this is the Moon Dragon, I hope you all can clearly see, they are on either side of me as you know," the Crystal Dragon introduced.

"Anyway, we together are the guardians of a very expensive and shiny crystal that a few teenagers and an adult robbed from a cave in the lower part of the mountain," the Crystal Dragon explained. "Therefore, it is our job to keep it safe and in place," the Crystal Dragon said. "Everyone here understand?" the Crystal Dragon questioned.

There was a moment of silence, and the three dragons just sighed simultaneously and obviously, non-regretfully.

"All right, I am guessing it is time to wipe-out the human race for eternity!" The Sun Dragon cried. "Yeah, it will be fun," the Moon Dragon agreed.

"Stop!" A man in a combat suit stood on a tank on the other side of the open land behind Ian. "We have the entire military department in the continent right here, you know," he yelled at the top of his lungs. Four dozen more tanks rolled out of the fields.

With a startling moment, Ian realized the person was Mayor Mack. Apparently, he built up his courage to go hunt for Ian and his crew.

"Oh, I forgot, we also have the air force patrolling the area just to make sure there are not going to be any more threats. I want to tell you that, all this time we were also trying to recapture these VIPs that were alleged bombers convicted of destroying a five-star hotel, the most famous of this city called Tad," he spoke smoothly despite his double-chin.

Mayor Mack pointed at Ian and his friends, making the dragons turn their heads sideways to see them. "I heard that these VIPs have been also convicted of stealing your precious crystal," Mayor Mack exclaimed.

At that moment, the first few fighter jets appeared in a formation of a triangle, going straight towards the Sun Dragon's left wing. They left clear trajectories in the sky.

But the Moon Dragon shrieked, and the Sun Dragon leaned backwards as a rocket missed his wing by a foot or two.

The Crystal Dragon shot crystal spikes and shards at the fighter jets. One was nailed in the underside. Another got pierced in the metal near the cockpit, smoke flying out. A third jet lost an entire front half of itself. The rest of the fighter jets went down except for one.

The still-flying fighter jet loosened another missile that shot like a torpedo at the Moon Dragon. It wiggled its wings and went diving toward the clump of tanks on the ground.

Ian watched as the Moon Dragon landed on a tank in the front row, smashing it to bits. It started slashing up more tanks. Ian saw the Moon Dragon picked up one, tossed it into the air, and punched a hole in its turret while it still spun in midair. Metal scraps and parts rained onto the open land.

Ian glanced at the ground, seeing another silhouette. It must be either the Sun Dragon or the

Crystal Dragon. Ian hastily looked up, realizing it was neither.

The same fighter jet that attempted to take down the Moon Dragon was rapidly spiraling down towards Ian and his friends with steam coming out of every opening in its aluminum. It was going to crash cockpit-first into the dirt and cause an explosion.

"Guys, let's run!" Drake screamed, making Ian's ear drums bounce from side to side, frantically trying to escape from the tight space.

"We have to get into the high grasslands now for shelter!" Joe cried. The terrain appeared beside the mountain. It sat next to a forest surrounding most of the mountain.

Ian and his friends had travelled all the way around just to walk on the thin and bumpy trail because Drake complained about gnats living in the trees. It wasted them another fifteen minutes or so. Joe had seemed like he was at the point of face-planting on dirt-covered ground and spending the night there.

The going-down jet started making unpleasant sounds that sounded like they were from an elephant's trunk.

Ian ran out of the silhouette's boundaries, trying to pull Alexis along, but she remained right in the center of the silhouette.

Ian whisked around and saw that Drake was also trying to pull Alexis out of the area the jet was going to crash into. Drake too turned around and his facial expression slowly changed at first sight.

"Come on, let me have a turn to be the hero for Alexis," Drake spoke demandingly. "You, Ian, should stop saving her all the time," Drake rolled his eyes. "I never got a turn!" Drake stomped his foot. "I never got a chance!" Drake yelled again, adamantly.

"Why haven't you let me join the fun and excitement? Is the reason why you chose me to be your best friend was because I had the lowest chance to steal your dream girl?" "You could have picked Josh to be your best friend," Drake cried. Ian grinded his teeth.

"I don't think your attitude is that great right now, it must have been addled lately because….." "Of course," Drake literally screamed while he yelled, "you baffled my emotions, you corrupted me not with force, but with actions," he replied.

"Drake! Ian! Get over here right now!" Joe called from somewhere in the distance. "The jet is on about to crash! Can one of you just let go?" Joe said and inquired.

Alexis seemed dazed as she squinted at the sky. She appeared to look like a puppet about to have her arms pulled off. Ian thought of the stress he felt back at the hotel when The Breaker was about to smash him with such force that all Ian's teeth was about to fly out.

Drake grinned at Ian. "It doesn't matter as long all three of us die together at the same time." Ian locked eyes with him and mouthed, fine. He stretched out his palm, letting Alexis' hand fall in a crescent.

Ian sprinted to the high grasslands, too humiliated to look back. He knew trouble was coming his way, on the path that he had to walk.

They had ran into The Haunter's minions, police officers, and S.W.A.T. sergeants. But now Ian even had to start dealing with his own best friend which he exchanged food (which were already tainted with both of their saliva) with and squeezed mustard sauce on.

Ian felt a sort of emptiness inside of him like he usually did when things got tough and of course…embarrassing. Ian thought of hiding underground as the three dragons took over the world. He contemplated on it.

There was a mighty roar, and the Sun Dragon touched down in front of the remaining tanks that survived the Moon Dragon, who flew towards the Crystal Dragon for different orders.

The Sun Dragon eyed Mayor Mack and sent a blast of nuclear energy out of its mouth. A fourth of the tanks disappeared in the dragon's stinging breath, but Mayor Mack managed to make it out the circumference before it hit.

He jumped onto another tank that went scurrying away. Mayor Mack scrambled up but belly-flopped on it right after he lost his balance.

The Sun Dragon continued sending out blasts of nuclear energy as the backup tanks attempted to injure the dragon with their built-in four-barreled firers, rolling all around with their wheels.

Chapter Nineteen: The Finally-Known Kid

Suddenly, the crystal Ian was holding just swung into the void. It must have been Flix, Ian thought. You else would? Ian's hand went to his pocket, where he shove out his Shadow-Contact gift and pressed the only button on it, used to call for help in an emergency. Flix materialized in front of Ian with a worried countenance.

"Where's the crystal, where's it?" Ian demanded. "I was about to ask you that!" Flix exclaimed. "Didn't you take it from my cuddled hands?" Ian inquired, glaring at Flix. "No! Trust me, Ian, someone who was in the shadows took it straight out of without permission," Flix said, still apprehensive. "It wasn't any of my kind, I couldn't sense them," he quickly added.

"Then you could it be if it wasn't anyone who grew up as a Shadow Clan figure?" Ian wondered. "Well," Flix started, "I did sense a human being walk right through that gap over there where your four discovered a cave and got the crystal," Flix considered. He also pointed his complex finger at the spot.

"Oh yeah, I should check it out!" Ian exclaimed. Flix nodded agreement. "Fine, but don't feel too adventurous or you will take too long in the cave and….." Flix hesitated, but Ian ignored him. "I'll be fine," Ian concluded.

With that, he sprinted to the opening and ducked through it. Ian then saw a figure on the other side of the lake where the crystal had been. He seemed to be on the verge of breaking through the fallen stalactites and settling the crystal back down onto the raised platform.

"Hey, get back over here and hand over the crystal," Ian cried. The figure seemed to not here him, but Ian knew he sure could because of the echoes off the cavern walls.

Ian glanced at the surface of the lake, seeing through it with clarity. Could I swim in it? Were there any jellyfish that sting? What was the temperature of the water for the first few feet? Ian thought.

He no doubt knew that he wouldn't swim in it even though the water looked so clean. But how could he get across without the wooden boat? He contemplated for several seconds and then had an idea that was too obvious.

His grappling hook! It was Ian's favorite utility he ever received despite after the midair bumping-around situation.

Ian took a glimpse at his plate of buttons and pressed a silver one as he pointed his Wrist Striker in the direction he wanted it to go. A metal claw sprang into the air, and in the blink of an eye, it clung onto the thickest stalactite that helped make up the fence blocking the path to the raised platform.

Ian zipped through the air of the cold cave. He kept his eyes from getting dizzy by trying to focus on what the person at the far side of the lake was doing.

The mysterious figure suddenly did something crazy that Ian screamed, "No! Don't do that!" The figure had intentionally threw the crystal at the stalactites that resembled a wall. The crystal broke through them, forming a hole.

Ian urged the cord that transported him to give him a boost before the person on the other side of the lake did anything even more insane. It didn't really work, but Ian still got himself to go by an increased 4mph.

He got closer and closer, realizing the figure was a short human being. Ian anticipated where he was going to land. He saw that it was the thick stalactite that the person had not yet broken. Ian twisted as he descended, writhing and wiggling.

He knew going SLAM into limestone wasn't a good idea.

Ian did his best and ended SMACK into the human being. He scrambled up and realized the person was a kid, the same one they found on the plane that went down. Ian put a hand to his heart and pursed his lips.

"What do you think you are doing with that crystal? It's not a toy as you know. Now trudge back to the boat and wait for me there as I check for any scratches you might have made with those long and disgusting nails of yours!" Ian summarized.

Surprisingly, the kid spoke back with no hesitations. "I have come back to retrieve my memory. All I remembered was how I died." Ian admonished him.

"Listen kid, this is no hide-and-seek game we are playing. This is serious, we can't leave it behind or lose it," Ian spoke slowly. "NO! What I said wasn't some kind of jocularity!" Ian was surprised the kid knew that word.

"You sound and seem like you should be several years older!" Ian considered. "Yeah right? The only thing I recall was having a life before jumping off a bridge in the center of a forest," the kid exclaimed.

"What? I'm bewildered." Ian stuttered and paused. "Oh, oh, okay, I-I just know a person who did the same thing of plunging off a bridge because of creatures called Zartees that ran at us," Ian said. "Really," the kid tried reading Ian's thoughts and seemed very successful after a few seconds.

Ian changed the subject. "So, if you are claiming that you died, how did you resurrect? And did you recall anyone there with you before you died?" Ian inquired curiously. "I just woke up in a public bathroom in the city of Yart," he replied. "In a supermarket," the kid added. "And no, I simply forgot that anybody was there the moment before I died." Ian started back-stepping away.

"Please, don't be afraid of what I speak." Ian was really getting scared of this kid who he had no idea was. Ian didn't even know what his name was, the simplest information that wouldn't give out too much identity.

"Um, hey, do you happen to have a name that you might remember?" Ian questioned. "No," the kid answered smoothly. Ian groaned, "Then tell me how you are going to get your memory back in a cave with a crystal."

"First off, as I woke up in a stall, I felt a dragging sensation as if it was reaching from the far corner of the northwest. So, when I took a step towards the West, I couldn't turn back around to walk east. After I watched the whole entire video of Chain of Cars Chase through Expressway, I wondered what was up with the driver and the passengers."

"Then, when we first met on the plane, I knew my instincts were right about something important I needed to retrieve. But instead of being conscious, you punched me in the face, and I went into a coma for a couple days!" "Oh, sorry about that, continue," Ian urged, completely waving away the question of why the kid started attacking them. "Teach me how you bursts out of the shadows," Ian begged.

"As I sat in the shadows, waiting as you all had fun, several Shadow Clan citizens came by and saw me just sitting there and passing time. They took pity on me and taught me how to break out of the shadows. I thanked them," the kid blurted out quickly. "There, you happy now?" He asked.

"I'm happy but not satisfied," Ian responded. "But my question is, how would you get your memory back here?" Ian inquired.

"What I was thinking, was that the crystal must have some sort of power in it that could cure my memory lost," the kid replied. "Hold out your hand and I will put the crystal on it," he said, "do it!" Ian shook, amazed to be taking orders from a three-year old.

Ian stretched out his hands and felt a cold and heavy object settled on his left hand. The kid looked through it at Ian's face as he held it up. Apparently, his eyes started widening. The kid magically grew a whole foot and seemed to get buffer. Ian was both shocked and stunned at the result. It was Jarret.

Chapter Twenty: The Dragon Take-Outing

Happiness embraced Ian so well that he fell to his knees and hugged Jarret's legs. It wasn't the best long-time-no-see greeting, but Jarret seemed to love it. What an interesting first-moment reunion!

Ian got up without stumbling and sobbed tears of joy. He wiped his eyes with the back of his hands and hugged Jarret very tightly. Ian stopped right after Jarret led out a strangled choke.

"Hey big cousin, I am back from the dead!" Jarret exclaimed. Ian was so caught up in the idea that Jarret was really there that he didn't even want to question him about his resurrection. Ian just wanted to celebrate for a whole month that Jarret was alive. It felt like a scar that Ian had for years slowly burned away.

Ian got so caught up in his own emotions that Jarret had to interrupt his moment of cheerfulness. "Um, uh, don't you have friends outdoors now on a battle field?" Ian completely lost his enthusiasm. "Right, oh no, the dragons!" Ian tore off his g-hook from the stalactite and hurried to the wooden boat.

Jarret hustled too. Ian hurtled the railing of the boat and landed in sitting position, causing the boat to tilt. Jarret hopped in and volunteered to take the paddle. "No!" Ian cried. "I need to do it, my friends are out there, and I should be the one able to keep track of the speed we go on this boat."

Ian paddled ferociously, flinging water into Jarret's eyes. "Wow, I don't remember feeling fresh water on my cheeks," Jarret muttered. After half-way across the river, Ian started to lose energy and paddled at a moderate speed.

He inquired, "Hey Jarret, I thought this boat sank with a column pushing it down through the depths." "Apparently, when the crystal scraped it, the whole thing just evaporated and became smoke with a PUFF!" Jarret answered. "What?" Ian yelled, a tad too loud, his voice reverberating off the wall. "Yeah, I'm not joking," Jarret spoke non-reluctantly.

"But then, how was it still on the surface for a long time?" Ian questioned. "Must have been the weight, the boat had supported the column with ease. Judging by the size of the column, it must have been true and a fact," Jarret considered.

They finally reached the shoreline, the boat halting by itself. Ian and Jarret stepped out of the boat and started sprinting to the gap where a sun's ray shone through.

Ian dove out of the cave into the mid-afternoon environment. Jarret however, stepped out of the cave with caution. Ian adjusted his eyes to see what was occurring.

Only a fourth of the deployed tanks still were in one piece. Ian's eyes went into finding mode to search for his friends. He spotted them backing-up into a tree as the Moon Dragon slowly crawled at them, its mouth open wide, ready to strike at any moment.

Ian tried screaming at the Moon Dragon so it would avert its eyes and settle them on him instead. But the Moon Dragon wasn't really a fool that could be easily tricked after all.

Joe raised his staff like a batter as the dragon spat out a meteor the size of a mansion. It whirled in the air with black smoke surrounding it as Joe waited for impact.

The meteor hit his staff, causing him to slide backwards, creating a straight line in the dirt. Joe was resilient and smacked the meteor back at the Moon Dragon. As the first meteor bounced back at the Moon Dragon, he slammed it back at Joe with the side of its head, right below its eye socket.

It continued like a game of ping pong. After only a minute and a half, Joe started trying to catch his breath. Ian knew Joe was losing his energy as big drops of sweat fell to the dirt ground. Ian suddenly had an idea where there was a contingency the Moon Dragon might be tricked finally.

"Hey, leather-sewed-in face! More fighter jets have arrived and are bombing your boss, the Crystal Dragon!" Ian shouted. The dragon actually took a glimpse at the sky, turning its head around.

Joe acted as quickly as he could. He wacked an incoming meteor back at the dragon's belly with a grunt. The meteor twirled back at the Moon Dragon and smashed into its tummy.

The Moon Dragon's head twisted around as it disintegrated into gray sand. His limbs, organs, belly, and tail broke down into ash which the wind swept away into space.

Ian watched patiently with both excitement and horror. Joe was staring at the ground, his chest elevating and going down. Drake sat against a tree with a relieved expression. Alexis was the only one who seemed as if she was still concerned about what was occurring around them.

Ian took Jarret's wrist and started running to his friends on the other side of the high grasslands. He wondered what the other two dragons were thinking of. They must be very angry.

Ian heard a noisy tank rumble towards him from a distance. He flew around and saw that it was the only tank still there. Mayor Mack perched on top of it and yelled, "I have got you now, VIP, there won't be any more exceptions as this tank charges at you. Begone!"

The battle vehicle accelerated right towards Ian. He could see the Sun and Crystal Dragon hovering over the tank like drones in spying mode.

WABAM!!! The tank flipped frontwards a few times. Mayor Mack had apparently jumped off the top before the nuclear blast came in. Both dragons touched down on the ground and kicked at the rubble.

"Man-made stuff are so cheap!" the Crystal Dragon spat. "Yeah, right?" the Sun Dragon agreed. They started picking at the wreckage until the Sun Dragon lifted up a familiar-looking figure with its tail.

Mayor Mack appeared with a sick-looking face. The Crystal Dragon glanced at him and said, "Well, well, well, I don't think we need your

171

presence anymore!" Mayor Mack started to seem very anxious. "Do I get the honors?" the Sun Dragon inquired. "Yes, he shall make up for the Moon Dragon's death. Let our revenge be accomplished," the Crystal Dragon cried.

The Sun Dragon twirled its tail. "Goodbye, old friend," the dragon said sarcastically. "Enjoy a nice cool moment of flying without parachutes, very few people ever dare to experience it, they are usually mad and mental," the Crystal Dragon spoke and noted.

Mayor Mack flew into the air, his hair obscuring part of the horizon. He went higher than the mountain and disappeared in the clouds. Ian's own mucus instantly tasted like raw fish.

"Ian, Ian, are you okay?" Alexis ran to meet him in the center of the open land with Drake behind. "Yeah!" Ian trembled. "Listen," Alexis ordered, "we have to get out of here." "But…." "I know, Ian," Alexis said, "it is almost impossible, but we should do this for our lives and our future," she pointed out. "Hey, no, move!" Drake shouted.

Ian saw yet another silhouette and tackled Alexis, rolling out of its boundaries. But a section of his shirt was still in it. A gigantic foot came down, ripping off Ian's most admired shirt.

Alexis found her hand on Ian's bare chest and she quickly slid it off. Ian scrambled up with Drake looking at them with a hand cupped over his mouth. Joe sprinted over and did the same. Alexis sighed, Ian groaned.

But suddenly, there was another ear-damaging roar and a claw appeared right in front of Alexis and flicked Joe into the forest behind them.

For a heart-stopping split second, Ian thought he had to tackle Alexis again to get her out of danger. Drake also reacted but also froze in the middle of the process.

The Sun Dragon bent low and gave Ian the evil-eye as another claw threw Drake and Alexis into the forest. Ian could almost hear the dragon chuckling hysterically as Ian, himself, screamed.

The Crystal Dragon had apparently went back to the top-half-sliced-off mountain's rim and perched calmly there like it was watching television without a remote control during free time.

Ian got crazily mad. As the Sun Dragon's lips parted, revealing its stained teeth, Ian did the unbelievable.

He dove into its mouth and belly-slid down its throat as he glanced at his Wrist Striker and pressed the haywire-fire-blasting button.

Bolts of red and blue shot randomly at the insides of the Sun Dragon.

Ian kept his eyes shut as he journeyed through its digestive system. It felt like an endless dark and very slimy water slide. Ian's skin slowly became wrinkled. He felt as if levitating for several hours (they were really minutes).

Ian suddenly breathed fresh air and plummeted. He wondered if falling to his death or just finishing himself off was a better way to die. No matter what, each option that popped into Ian's mind had an equal amount of stress that smoldered inside him. Ian finally decided to just let gravity take his life, but he still wanted to defy it.

Ian heard the sound of more fighter jets as he landed on a very bouncy trampoline. He went up, he went down. But Ian was so toughened up that he didn't want to stop fighting.

Ian hopped off the trampoline, surprising a few armless corps. He marched over to where Jarret was hiding, by the base of the mountain. "Give the crystal to me, I need it," he said. Jarret obeyed him and handed it over.

Ian turned around and faced the Crystal Dragon with the crystal held high on his palm, distracting the dragon from the planes.

"You want it? Have it!" The dragon dove down without a respond. He went straight at Ian. Ian was prepared to punch the dragon's nostrils so its snout would spill out. He wasn't afraid anymore, at least right at that moment.

But as the dragon's snout got within arm's length, there was a flash of purple, and the dragon just disappeared in thin air.

Ian looked up at the crystal. It was rapidly careening and the flat-bottom was also getting very hot. Ian dropped it. He suddenly understood why there were symptoms. The Crystal Dragon had been sucked in, it was the best conclusion he could make of it.

Chapter Twenty-One: A New Beginning

Later that day, Ian and his friends got to ride in an army truck. They sat in the backseats as the driver told them about his own experience as a soldier.

After an hour or two, they arrived at Roost, the capital of the continent. Ian and Drake together helped fit the crystal into the empty opening at the top of Joe's staff. It took some effort, but it was an excellent place to keep it.

When they got off, Alexis suggested that Ian call his mom right away with a public phone. They walked across the street to a phone stall. Joe took out a 25 cents coin from his pocket and slid it in, through the slot.

Ian dialed his home phone number and Lorry Lanterncup's voice came. "Hello, may I ask, who is this?" She was about to hang up but Ian spoke swiftly.

"Hey mom, we survived getting the crystal," he said. Lorry thanked God and talked back. "Ian, you and your friends are amazing! What happened?" Lorry inquired.

So Ian told her just about everything including making friends with Flix. Lorry had recalled watching the news and seeing the five-star hotel in ruins. Ian didn't summarize the whole story, but he did pretty much told her every move they made as Joe kept sliding more coins into the slot.

When Ian finished, Lorry just sighed. "So mom, can we go home now?" Ian asked gratefully. "No," she responded with a trace of despair. "There is a part two," Lorry blurted out. "You will have to travel all the way to the east coast where Shadow Clan inhabits to deliver the crystal to them." "Oh, my," Ian replied. "Yeah, but it is the only way to revive the friendship between our two races." "Ok mom, we will do it," Ian said. "Remember, I love you," Lorry answered, and Ian hung up.

They browsed around town. Apparently the news of teens and an adult destroying two dragons and sucking one into a crystal had gone viral.

All the people they passed had given them either hand-shakes or fists bumps. One guy even handed out free airline tickets to them without reluctance.

Ian and his friends strolled to the airport and quickly went through check-in and security to catch their flight to Terp.

They at last made it on time to their gate, number 26. "We should wash our hands after so much germs!" Joe suggested, even though his common sense concept was poor. "Oh yes," they responded.

They finally boarded the passenger plane after they all got out of the restrooms.

✳✳✳

The plane quickly took off from the runway and ascended into the sky.

"Well, we did it!" Alexis said brightly while Drake was in the back using the lavatory. "Yeah," Ian couldn't say more after what he did to the Sun and Crystal Dragon. Alexis had told him about the event in her own perspective.

"I think I'm going to sleep," Alexis yawned, her hand over her mouth. Alexis' head drooped onto her shoulder, which was a centimeter from Ian's.

Ian smirked for the first time in a week and a half. "What's up?" Joe called from the seat behind him. "Nothing," Ian said, but he couldn't abstain himself from grinning. "Ok," Joe concluded.

It was only 45 minutes when they reached the sea. Ian looked out the window for a clear view.

But the scene was photo-bombed. Out came an enormous green and brown creature that loomed out of the water.

Acknowledgements

I wouldn't have taken this book to completion if it weren't for a few colleagues who worked diligently by my side.

I'll first like to thank my mom. She had encouraged me not to give up the process of this story when errors occurred and I lost several pages off fully-written words. Secondly, I had love to thank my dad too. He taught me how to use Microsoft Word. My dad also did the front page. He took pictures of the crystal with different backgrounds and let me/mom choose one photo out of them (it was hard because they all appeared flawless). Overall, my parents have guided and supported me emotionally.

Another couple people who given me boosts on the story were Jeremy Hefner and my school friend Alex. I hardly know Jeremy Hefner, but he came to my church one Sunday and preached especially with difficult words. Jeremy inspired me. As for Alex, he gave me advice and fresh ideas whenever I asked for them. Alex never forced me to accept each of his ideas, instead, he let me choose.

Mostly, I'll want to thank God, Yahweh, for lending me such a talent when I was born. Remember, God is a gift-giver to everyone!!

Description: Thirteen-year-old boy named Ian Lanterncup gets distressed and grieved after the losing his father. He has no choice but to go back to school. He saves the school bully and flees for his life.

They barely make it back home until Lorry Lanterncup, Ian's mom, gives them a quest to complete. She speaks to them about a crystal that can restore peace with another race. It supposedly hid in the far-northwest where the tallest point of the world was.

In this hilarious short novel, Ian and his friends collide with evil's minions the entire way. But mankind also joins in when destruction of their own society occurs.

As arduous as that, Ian Lanterncup faces issues alone including voices in his head and getting quarrelsome with his best friend, Drake. But can Ian withstand vast obstruction when unusual times are present??